The Condor's Feather

The Condor's Feather

Margaret Muir

ROBERT HALE · LONDON

ISBN 978-0-7090-8822-6

Robert Hale Limited
Clerkenwell House
Clerkenwell Green
London EC1R 0HT

www.halebooks.com

2 4 6 8 10 9 7 5 3 1

In memory of my sister Barbara Leak whose wonderful work for
women with breast cancer will never be forgotten.

Typeset in 11½/16pt Palatino
by Derek Doyle & Associates, Shaw Heath
Printed in Great Britain by
the MPG Books Group, Bodmin and King's Lynn

ACKNOWLEDGEMENTS

When I first visited South America, I learned of the adventures of Lady Florence Dixie. In 1878, aged twenty-one, this young English aristocrat embarked on a remarkable ride across the pampas of Patagonia.

Reading her story inspired me to write this book.

I must also acknowledge Charles Darwin, Julius Beerbohm, and George C Musters – the true-life adventurers who recorded their remarkable experiences in this inhospitable region. In accordance with their published works, I have adopted the old names of Buenos Ayres and Monte Video. Finally, my thanks to Hester Davonport for her help in directing my research, and to Susanna Rogers and Marion Collins for their valuable comments and advice.

CHAPTER 1

Huntingley – 1885

'Madam, you are incorrigible!'

'And you are a pompous ass, Brother dear!'

'What is wrong with you, Cynthia?'

'Nothing,' she replied sweetly.

Horatio Beresford scowled at his younger sister, then drained the contents of his glass as if it were water. 'Good God, woman, you must be soft in the head! Your behaviour is – to say the least – unacceptable, nay, even reprehensible.'

Sinking gracefully to the floor in a cross-legged position, Cynthia Beresford bunched her skirt and petticoats above her stockinged knees, poked out her chin and, with her spine straight as a plumb-line, sat motionless, her hands resting lightly on her head.

'See what I mean!' he growled, glaring at her. 'Your behaviour! Your mannerisms! You are a. . . .'

Cynthia pursed her lips and exhaled slowly. 'I am a . . . what?' she asked calmly.

Shaking his head, her brother refilled his glass. 'You realize that last weekend everyone at the meet was talking about you. And as if it was not irksome enough to see you wearing a pair of men's breeches – and, I might add, riding the tallest mount in the stable – but to see you sitting astride – riding like a man! How undignified. How embarrassing. I overheard Amanda Trenby tell her niece that you completely lacked any semblance of breeding and, if it were not for the fact you have father's aquiline nose, she would have doubted you were a Beresford at all.'

'Amanda Trenby should learn to lower her voice and keep her comments to herself. Besides I wouldn't be surprised if *she* was conceived on the wrong side of the blanket.'

'Cynthia!'

'Thia!' she retorted. 'You know I hate it when you address me as Cynthia. You only do it to annoy me.'

'Damn you, madam. It is your name after all. What has got into you these days? Since the papers started publishing your letters, you think you have the right to say and do exactly as you please. You should consider your position. Consider Father's position! Consider my position! How dare you pen scathing criticism of some of the centuries' old laws of England! As to your opinions on women's rights, female suffrage and issues relating to the working classes. . . ! How do you think Father feels when he is in the House?'

'I am sure Papa doesn't mind a jot, and no doubt the malicious gossip whispered between the Members helps to keep the old peers awake during those tediously long sittings.'

Horatio shook his head and poured himself another ample measure of French brandy. 'You are disrespectful and impudent! As to putting your outlandish notions on paper. . . !' He clenched his teeth. 'It amazes me that respectable newspapers print such drivel. I was flabbergasted when I noted *The Times* had published another of your lengthy epistles only last week. Gracious! What is the country coming to?'

'My very point, Horatio.' She glanced at him, grinning slightly. 'As to my letters – the content is hardly drivel. I express an opinion and I am as entitled to my opinion as much as you are to yours.'

'Entitled within the confines of these walls, maybe, but beyond Huntingley. . . .' His eyebrows raised halfway to his receding hair-line. 'It is time you kept your views to yourself and started behaving in the manner befitting your breeding. I do not know why you are so averse to following genteel pursuits as other ladies do. What is wrong with tapestry, or painting, or croquet? I cannot comprehend why you delight in standing in the middle of the river hurling a line at a fish which has no intention of being caught, or sitting in a thicket for hours watching birds' eggs going rotten in a nest. Your behaviour is truly weird and I blame it on the evil books you read.'

Thia dropped her hands to her lap. Resting them palm uppermost, she glanced at her brother who was swaying back and forth in front of the fireplace.

'Ha!' he snorted defiantly, a supercilious sneer twisting the corners of his mouth. 'You didn't think I knew about them, did you?'

'What books I choose to read is no business of yours.'

'As the heir of Huntingley, I make it my business to know everything that goes on in this house, and the books which you secrete away in your bedroom are—'

'—are classics.'

'That is not what I would call them. Goodness, Cynthia, I would be embarrassed to show those volumes to some of the gentlemen at the meet.'

'I would think those friends of yours have been reading the literature in question since before hair started sprouting from

9

their armpits. Besides, there would not be one man amongst them who I would call a real gentleman.'

'I cannot believe the words that utter from your mouth!'

Thia smiled innocently. 'But, Horatio, I am only doing what you previously suggested I should do.'

He looked at her, aghast. 'And what, pray, is that? I never asked you ride like a man, or read such diabolical rubbish!'

Touching her temple, Thia smiled graciously. 'Ah, but wasn't it you who said I should improve my mind by reading the French classics?'

'Damn you, Cynthia! You know damn well that I meant Voltaire or Rousseau, not the surrealistic ramblings of a reprobate such as the Marquis de Sade.'

Thia grinned. 'You amaze me, Brother. I didn't know you were familiar with the Marquis's work.'

'Cynthia,'

'Thia, if you please. Or perhaps you would prefer to call me Juliette?'

'Cynthia!'

'Or Justine!' she replied, trying hard to control her desire to smile.

'Cynthia, enough! You are totally audacious and incorrigible! Are you trying to bring this family into disrepute and make me into a laughing stock?'

'I hardly think that is necessary, Brother; you seem to be doing the job perfectly admirably without my help. Now, would you kindly refrain from raising your voice? The atmosphere is not conducive to my meditation.'

As Thia closed her eyes, a flash of burning brandy whooshed up the chimney and the Waterford balloon exploded into a thousand shards on the blue tiled hearth. One of the large Newfoundland dogs which had been stretched out on the Indian rug, sidled surreptitiously to the far side of the sofa.

'Damn your meditations, madam! And damn you. If I were not a gentleman I would bind you and give you a thrashing.'

'Ah, remind me, was that in *Justine* or *Juliette*? No doubt you found the books enlightening!'

'You are no better than a gutter-snipe. You do nothing to enhance the family name and it will give me the greatest pleasure when you leave Huntingley.'

Picking up a fresh glass, the elder son of the Beresford family splashed another liberal serving of spirit into it, swirling the bronze liquid around the glass before taking a mouthful. 'I can see why you are not married,' he stated, not allowing time for a response. 'But I will recommend to Father that he finds you a husband as soon as possible. Or better still, why don't I find one? Let me think, who do I really hate that I can foist you on to? Someone truly despicable.' His eyes glistened, as he considered the possibilities. 'How about that cad with the cleft palate, Thurswhistle. Huh! The man cannot even pronounce his own name? Perhaps he will transport you abroad – to Calcutta or Cairo. And perhaps, if I am really fortunate, the ship will sink and you will drown while you are in transit. Failing that, perhaps when you are there you will contract cholera or yellow fever or even bubonic plague. In fact,' he added, 'I would recommend he takes you to Panama. I understand that is an inhospitable, disease-ridden place. Yes, I wholeheartedly suggest you go there!'

'Thank you, Horatio, I will consider it. But would it not be better if I venture there alone? Then there will be a greater chance of me being set upon by brigands and ravished, or hacked to pieces by inhospitable natives.'

'No more than you deserve, Sister, dear.'

Oblivious to his cynicism, Thia closed her eyes, took a deep breath and hummed on a single note.

'My problem is,' he scoffed, 'that I doubt even my worst enemy would be interested in you. Do you realize you will probably never marry? I declare you will die a spinster – dried up in both mind and body.'

'Dry as a leaf, Brother, dear. So dry in fact, the softest zephyr will lift me from the ground and carry me far away from this place.'

'The further away the better!' he shouted, heading for the door.

The two dogs pricked up their ears but did not follow.

As he stormed out, he would have collided with his father had Lord Beresford not stepped to one side. Horatio slowed marginally to acknowledge him. 'Father,' he said, bustling through before veering towards Huntingley' s west wing and the privacy of his private drawing-room.

'I thought I heard raised voices,' Lord Beresford said, quietly closing the double doors. 'Were you two arguing again?'

'Of course not, Papa. We were discussing French literature!'

A wry smile curled on the old man's lips, as he leaned down and placed a kiss on his daughter's forehead.

'I think you take a perverse delight in goading your brother.'

'But he provides such wonderful sport, Papa.'

'And, you, my dear Thia, are like the hounds – once you have the scent, you follow the prey until the unfortunate beast is cornered and driven to distraction. I think you do not know when to give up.' Relaxing into the wing chair, Lord Beresford sighed. 'I sometimes find it hard to believe that you two had the same mother, God bless her soul. You are so

12

different – and so is Algernon too.'

Thia straightened the front of her gown, shook the flounce over her knees and released the lace frills around her cuffs which she had tucked back into her sleeve. Sliding along the floor in order to be closer to her father, she looked up at him with a slightly pained quizzical expression. 'Horrie certainly did not get his exasperating nature from you, Papa. And from what you have told me of Mama, I cannot imagine it was from her either.'

The old man inhaled deeply. 'I'm afraid I must admit it was though. Your mother was a truly remarkable woman; intelligent, engaging, creative, but at the same time, she could be exasperating and stubborn, and intolerant of the demands which society placed upon her.' He paused. 'My dear, Thia, you and your brother, Horatio, have inherited her strong characteristics between you, while her soft and gentle qualities were bestowed on your brother, Algy.'

'But surely Mama was never as spiteful as Horrie often appears to be?'

'Unfortunately, for the twelve years Horatio was the only child in the house, he was completely spoiled. During that time, he was doted on by both your mother and I, and was allowed to do virtually anything he wanted. Unfortunately that changed the day you and Algy were born and from then on he regarded you both as a threat to his position.'

'But he is so very arrogant at times. Not at all like you, Papa. Surely Mama's temperament was not like that.'

'No, it was not. I think your brother's arrogance was instilled in him by a series of nannies and haughty tutors. I could never comprehend why your mama chose some of them, but I always left those matters to her and never argued with her choice. As I have told you, she was a strong woman

13

with bold, forthright ideas. She ran the house most efficiently and took complete charge of Horatio's upbringing. With hindsight, I should have taken a firmer hand. Now I find it regrettable that he resents and blames you and Algy for your Mama's death.'

Thia squeezed her father's hand. 'Poor, dear, Papa,' she said. 'You have never resented Algy and me, as Horrie does, have you?'

'Resented?' The old man said, suddenly appearing older than his sixty years. 'That is a foolish question. Why should I hold any resentment against you, my dear?'

Thia rested her cheek on his hand and spoke softly. 'Horatio says my actions and words embarrass you. If they do, I will stop. I can change my ways.'

The elderly man regarded his daughter, his wistful eyes ready to spill their moisture. 'Had you known your mother, you would not have asked that question. You are so much like her,' he said, gazing at the life-sized oil painting hanging above the fireplace. 'It is uncanny. She had a certain boldness – a strength of character and courage which you have. Yet some pointed the finger and said she was uncouth. Said her actions were deliberately set to provoke or shock.'

'Is that what you thought, Papa?'

He smiled. 'Sometimes they were, but always in a cheeky or playful manner. She never hurt anyone intentionally. To me her very behaviour, her every mannerism, her grace and ease, these were the things which attracted me to her. She was so refreshing, so warm, so honest and she hated the confines which society dictated she should adhere to. She forever wanted to tear down the barriers which restrained her.'

'Then why didn't she?'

'She tried. Like you she wrote. She expressed her views in

14

no uncertain terms, but because society was more rigid forty years ago than it is today, she realized she could never succeed. Perhaps too, because she was married to a staid old fool like me she didn't try as hard as she could.'

'Papa, how can you say that?'

He squeezed her hand. 'Had your mother been born a man she would have been an adventurer, an explorer, a politician. She had tenacity and spirit. No obstacle would have stopped her. But, when Horatio was born, she veiled her desires. I think she purposely harnessed her free spirit. I watched it slip away. It evaporated like morning mist from a meadow.' He tilted his head to the picture. 'I never once asked her to change. I loved her exactly as she was with all her foibles and strange ways. She was so vibrant; different to any other woman I had ever met. She was freshness itself; like sun after rain; like the first snowdrop bursting from the frozen earth; like the first foot-prints across a carpet of fresh snow. So firm and positive,' he sighed. 'But like a footprint cut in a mat of snowflakes, I knew her spirit was something I could not hold on to forever. Then one day the snow melted. . . .' Lord Beresfield sniffed.

Looking into his rheumy eyes, Cynthia detected a plea for reassurance.

'What is it, Papa? Please tell me. Why are you sad?'

Lord Beresford held his hands towards the fire but the chimney was consuming the heat. He shivered involuntarily. 'Sometimes I hate this house,' he said. 'No, not hate, but feel it has a hold over me – a hold I cannot ever break free from. Sometimes I feel very lonely.'

'Papa, I have never heard you say such things before. I always thought you loved Huntingley. You speak so proudly of the family's heritage. I thought it was that which made you such a noble man. There is not one person on the estate who

15

does not love and respect you, and you have many friends both at Westminster and at your club.'

'My dearest, Thia,' he said, cupping her hands in his warm, marshmallow palms. 'There are certain things I should have said to you years ago, but I have never had the courage to reveal.'

'What is it, Papa? What is troubling you?'

Lord Beresford lifted his eyes and gazed around the room from the striped silk upholstered furnishings to the dark velvet curtains at the tall windows; to the exotic ebony bureau inlaid with mother of pearl and the faces of his gilt-framed ancestors gathered on the walls around the room. But none of them held his attention for more than a second and his eyes returned to the full-length portrait positioned above the mantelshelf. The young woman in the picture was strikingly handsome. Tall and confident. Her sea-blue gown reflected the colours of the room.

'How I miss your mother,' he said sadly.

Thia paused for a moment before repeating her question. Her tone quiet and cautious. 'Do you resent Algy and me for taking her from you?'

'My dearest Thia, it was not your birth which caused her death.'

'But I always thought—'

'What you thought was merely a myth – a satisfactory myth which I allowed to slide neatly into everyone's mind. A story which over the years has taken on reality, which everyone now accepts as the truth. I alone permitted it to happen. I never discouraged it. That was very wrong of me, was it not?'

'What do you mean, Papa? You speak of a myth. I do not understand.'

'It was a façade which allowed me to excuse myself from

blame.' Pain creased his already weary face, as he struggled to find adequate words. 'And it made your mother's death easier for me to accept. But I was wrong to let you go on thinking she died in childbirth. I realize that now. How old are you, Thia? Twenty-four, twenty-five?'

'This is my twenty-seventh year, Papa.'

He shook his head. 'Then I have carried this burden for almost twenty-seven years!'

'Dearest Papa, tell me about Mama. I will never repeat what you say.'

'I let her die. I let your dear mother die.'

Cynthia waited for a moment.

A tear trickled down her father's cheek.

'I don't understand,' she said.

Lord Beresford sighed. Finding the right words was not easy. 'After the strain of bearing you and Algy, your Mama never fully recovered. For several months she was unwell, but being stubborn, she hid her pain.' He smiled sadly. 'That was so typical of her. She was so independent, she did not even share her suffering with me. I remember in the afternoons when the troubles affected her, she would take to her chamber and give instructions she did not wish to be disturbed.'

'Please go on.'

'She died on the sixteenth of July. It was a Thursday. A lovely day. The sort of summer's day when everything in the garden comes alive, when everything is so fresh and the colours so vibrant. I remember that day as if it were yesterday.' He paused. 'After eating hardly anything for lunch your mama said she wanted to retire, but I insisted she step into the garden and walk with me for a while. I realized I was being selfish, but I needed her company. I wanted her to walk beside me, to stand together arm in arm and watch the gold-

17

fish swimming in the pond. I wanted to show her the masses of waterlilies which were in full bloom. Your mama loved their flowers.'

'Dear Papa.'

'I knew she was in pain, and I knew she agreed to accompany me for my sake. She always wanted to please me. Never disappoint me. But on that occasion, after we had wandered for a short while, she asked to be excused to go to her bedchamber. I accompanied her. I wanted to be with her, to comfort her. But she would not allow me into the room. She wanted to be alone. I felt hurt and left. When I returned to her door a few moments later, I was about to knock when I heard a strange gurgling sound.'

He sighed heavily. 'I didn't know she was dying. I had never heard the sound of death before. Pray God, I never hear it again! I thought she was sick and, like the fool I was, I listened for a moment then returned to the library and picked up a book.' Lord Beresford shook his head before continuing. 'I was sitting comfortably beside the window while your mother was dying. I was reading, Dante's *Divine Comedy*.' He shook his head. 'How ironical!'

'Oh, Papa. How terrible for you.'

'When her maid found her some hours later, she was cold and stiff. She was stretched out on the carpet with her head resting on her hands as though she was sleeping.'

Thia wiped her father's cheeks with her handkerchief. 'But it was not your fault she died. Why didn't you speak of this before, Papa? Why did you never tell any of us what really happened?'

'Because of my grief and guilt. Because I should have been there to help her, to summon the physician, perhaps save her, but also because I could not bear to think about her death. It was easier to let you grow thinking she had died when you were born.'

'Poor dear Papa.'

'Yet, as I have watched you grow from child to woman, I have seen so much of her in you. Your looks, your wiry brown curls, the fire in your hazel eyes, your smile, the way you walk or turn your head, but most of all your independent spirit.

'I often come into this room and gaze up at your mother's portrait. I need to remind myself she is no longer here. After twenty-seven years I still hear the rustle of her silk along the empty corridors. I smell her fragrance in my room. I hear the shuffle of her kid shoes tiptoeing around me as I drift into sleep – but when I open my eyes the room is always empty and she is not there.

'Sometimes I resent this house because it holds so many memories and I wish I was not here. Sometimes I feel the need to get away, far, far away but there is nowhere far enough that can take me from my guilt and memories.'

'Papa, you must put this sadness behind you. You have carried it too long. We should go away. Leave Huntingley and all the memories behind.'

'I could not leave Huntingley. This has been the family seat for over two hundred years.'

'Of course not, but for a while perhaps. A holiday. Six months? A year? Let us do it, Papa. Let us go away from here – you, me and Algy. I am sure Horatio will be happy to be master of Huntingley for a while.' Thia didn't wait for her father to answer. 'Yes, Papa, I think that is a wonderful notion. I would love to get away too. I really want to travel.'

Lord Beresford checked the time on his pocket watch for no particular reason. 'Perhaps a break would do me good,' he said, as he rose and strolled over to the large sepia globe sitting in front of one of the windows. 'We could revisit Paris or Rome. Or go to Venice. Venice is pleasant at any time of the year.'

Thia followed him. 'Papa, I want to get away from the seasonal travelling fraternity. They are boring, stuffy and stereotyped and so aristocratic.'

'But you must remember that is your birthright. It is something you should be proud of. Something the common people envy us for.'

'I am proud to be your daughter and to be part of this family. But I want to go somewhere new, exciting, and different.'

The old man spun the globe gently. 'North America. New York or Boston, perhaps?'

Thia frowned and studied the continents more closely. 'No,' she said bluntly, squatting to examine the southern hemisphere. 'Let us choose somewhere that hardly anyone else visits. A place where there are wide open spaces, clear skies and reeling eagles. Where rivers of ice creep down the sides of rugged mountains, and where rare flowers cast their seeds over thousands of miles of arid land. I have been reading about such a place.'

The glee in her eyes was evident as she traced her finger down the Andes Mountain Range from Peru in the north to the scattered remnants of broken land submerged in the sea at the very tip.

'Patagonia,' she squealed, 'Argentina, Chile, Tierra del Fuego. How exciting! The tail end of the earth. That is where we shall go.'

CHAPTER 2

The Hunt

Edmund Arkwright's mount, a chestnut stallion, glistened with the sheen of polished mahogany. The horse, he was leading, was a bay mare. Its foal trotted along beside in an ungainly fashion. As Huntingley's head groom rode beneath the stone archway, the row of white doves, decorating its span, lifted in unison and hovered a few feet above the arch, waiting for the horses to pass before returning to their perch.

The flapping feathers, beating on the afternoon air, accompanied the crunch of hoofs on the driveway and alerted the motley crowd gathered by the hand-pump in the centre of the stable yard. Turning towards the sounds, the faces soon revealed the likely consequences of the head groom's return. The urgent chatter ceased immediately. Grooms and stable hands shifted uneasily before hurrying back to the stables. Two maids lifted their skirts and dashed frantically across the courtyard, disappearing through the scullery door.

Jimmy Turner, the stable lad who had only recently been given a job at Huntingley, tugged his cap further down on his brow in a vain attempt to hide his identity, however, being only four feet eight inches tall he was easy to recognize. Grasping the handles of his empty barrow, he continued across the courtyard to the haystack. From the stable's entrance, one of the older grooms stepped out dusting down his sleeves and fastening the buttons on his jacket. He trotted across the cobblestones to meet his superior.

Arkwright looked at him disdainfully before handing him the reins of the horse he was leading. The Huntingley groom promptly led the mare into the stable, the foal trotting along-side it.

'All right! What's going on 'ere?' Arkwright shouted, directing his piercing stare at the youngest of the scullery maids. 'You! Get back to where you belong.'

The girl ran.

Then his gaze transferred to a face that was unfamiliar to him. The young woman was wearing a heavy brown corduroy skirt and, though it was a mild day, was holding a knitted shawl tightly to her chest. 'And who are you?'

'Aggie Turner,' she sniffed, craning her neck to look up at him. 'I'm Jimmy's ma, sir,' she said, bobbing fractionally, not knowing whether she was supposed to curtsy to the man in the saddle.

'Well, you ain't got no business 'ere. The lad's fine and while ever he works here, he belongs to Huntingley and there'll be no pestering from the likes of you. Now get out of my yard before I run you out!'

Rubbing the moisture from her eyes, Aggie looked up at him. The eyes she met were cold as ice and as sly as those of the grey gargoyles glaring down from Huntingley's stone gutters.

'But, sir, it's not for our Jimmy's sake I had to come 'ere. I had to see my aunty,' she begged softly. 'Matter of life or death, sir. I promise.'

The rider spurred his horse towards her. 'Get out of my yard, I said!'

By now the crowd had scattered. Only one other person remained in the yard. Confused and fearful, Aggie stumbled backwards into the arms of Cynthia Beresford's maid, Ethel Thoroughgood.

The older woman stepped to one side, folded her arms across her chest defiantly and looked directly into the man's face towering above her. As Arkwright jerked on the reins, the stallion snorted thrashing its head and mane.

'This ain't your yard, Ed Arkwright, any more than it's mine. And as I were at Huntingley long before you started shovelling horse muck, I guess I'm more entitled to be here than you.'

'We'll see what the master has to say about that. You!' he yelled, to the youth who appeared from one of the stalls. The hint of a smirk quickly dissolved from the boy's face. He hurried forward, rubbing his hands down the seat of his trousers before taking the stallion's bridle and allowing Arkwright to dismount.

'Saddle up Mr Horatio's hunter and a fresh mount for me. And be quick about it!' he ordered. 'As for you Miss Thoroughgood-for-nothing, I'll show you who's in charge around here. My master'll have something to say about this when I tell him.'

'That's right, go tittle-tattling to young Master Horatio.'

'You just wait until he's master of Huntingley. Then you'll not be littering up my courtyard with your snivelling relatives. I'll make sure of that!'

Ethel shook her head, turned her back on the rider and grabbed the young woman by the hand.

Uncertain of her situation, but with little alternative, the girl allowed herself to be dragged to the house. As they reached the door, the smack of Arkwright's riding crop against his leather boots did not check the older woman's resolve.

'Take no heed of him, Aggie,' she said, in loud voice. 'Come and wait in the kitchen, while I go speak with my mistress. She'll know what to do.'

'But I can't go inside. I don't belong in there. And I don't want to get you or our Jim in no trouble. I'm afraid that Mr Arkwright—'

'Hold your tongue, girl!' Ethel hissed, grasping the girl's arm and pulling her firmly through the scullery door.

Arkwright turned his back on the pair. Now the only sounds in the yard were those of his boots and the crack of his riding crop rapping across the leather. When he reached the pump he stopped and looked around. Slowly and deliberately he removed his white gloves, took off his hat and stroked his hand across his greasy hair.

'Damn women,' he said, under his breath. 'Huntingley is cursed with damn women!'

'You say the child disappeared yesterday?' Cynthia Beresford said kindly, to the distraught young mother.

'Yes, ma'am. Went off after breakfast and that was the last I saw of her. She never came home for her tea. She were gone all night but she weren't dressed for it. I can't bear to think what might have happened to her. She'll be frozen stiff by now, if not worse.'

Thoroughgood pulled a crumpled handkerchief from her cuff and handed it to her niece.

'I do not think she will be frozen as it is July and the nights have been remarkably warm,' Thia said. 'But there are other things to take into consideration. How old is she, Aggie?'

'Nearly six, ma'am.'

'Was she alone?'

'Aye, apart from her pup. She never went nowhere without him. Like a whippet, it is. She calls him Spot.'

'And do you have any idea where your daughter might have gone?'

'Aye, ma'am, I know only too well. She went off to Henley Woods. Said her and Spot were off searching for badgers.'

Cynthia Beresford turned to her maid. 'I shall require my riding clothes, Goody. I must speak with Lord Beresford. We must organize a search party. I'll arrange for someone to ride over to Ellery Lodge. Perhaps they will be able to spare a few men to help. It should be light until late this evening so there is a chance we will find her tonight, if we take the dogs.'

Aggie squealed, 'No, please, ma'am! Not the dogs! I've heard they tear a fox to shreds when they find it. Not the dogs, ma'am, I beg you.'

Thia touched the girl's shoulder. 'Don't worry, my dear. I don't intend to call out the hounds. I am referring to Bella and Byron, my own dog and Lord Beresford's. I can assure you, Aggie, they are as mild and gentle as spring lambs. And hopefully, they will lead us to your daughter.'

The look of panic still creased Aggie's tear-streaked face.

Her aunt grasped her hands. 'You listen to what my mistress is saying. It's a true fact, there be no more harm in one of them big dogs than in the great feather pillow on the master's bed.'

Thia turned her head, concealing her desire to smile. Though she was loath to admit it, she had to agree with her

maid's allusion. How many times as a girl had she fallen
asleep with her face nestled into the thick warm double-coat
of one of Huntingley's Newfoundlands? For her and her
brothers the massive dogs were more than mere pets and
playthings. They were a symbol – a part of their heritage
and had been for several generations. The Beresford family
had kept Newfoundlands from early in the century, the likeness of one of the original Newfoundlands being incorpo-
rated into the family crest. Thia visualized the shaggy-
haired dog on their coat of arms which hung on the wall
above the entrance to the long gallery. The heraldic crest
included a noble canine, one paw raised and a fish held in
its jowls. She considered Byron, her father's dog, was very
similar to the one depicted.

Thia smiled at the two women, a glint in her eye. 'I can
assure you, the dogs are a good deal heavier than a pillow
filled with duck-down.'

Thoroughgood nudged her niece. 'Are you listening to
what Miss Cynthia is saying?'

Aggie sniffed, nodded and tried to smile.

'Thank you, Goody,' Thia said. 'Now, I want you to go
home, Aggie. Do you live in the village?'

'Yes, ma'am. But I can't go back. I got to keep looking.'

'I understand your concern, but there is something I need
you to do. Go home and get a bundle of your daughter's
clothes.'

Aggie's brow furrowed. Turning to her aunt, she whispered,' She ain't got many clothes apart from what she was
wearing.'

'Does she wear a bonnet to church?' Thia asked.

'Of course, ma'am. Sunday mornings for chapel.'

'And does she have a bed of her own?'

Aggie looked puzzled. 'She's got a cot in the corner of the bedroom. Her Dad made the frame.'

'Then bring the bonnet and the blanket from her bed. We will need them. Wait by the pond on the village green. I shall be there in about an hour with a party to search for your daughter.'

Aggie bobbed a curtsy. 'Thank you, ma'am. Thank you ever so much.'

'Save your thanks. We haven't found her yet, Aggie.' Thia turned to her maid. 'Tell Jackson that Lord Beresford will be going riding immediately. I will tell my brother as I am sure he will want to come along.'

'Begging your pardon, ma'am, but I heard Mr Arkwright say that he and Mr Horatio were going straight out.'

'Then that is one less to worry about.' Thia turned, 'My breeches, Goody. No time to lose.'

Ethel Thoroughgood nodded, but her mistress didn't wait for the acknowledgment. 'You heard what my mistress said. Don't dilly-dally. Get a bundle together. If anyone can find the little lass it'll be Miss Cynthia.'

The pond on the edge of the green sparkled in the late afternoon sun. In the centre, a pair of ducks swam in lazy circles seemingly ignorant of the men who were squelching through the tangled reeds prodding the mud with long stakes.

Under the inn's swinging sign, their womenfolk had gathered, old and young, some holding babies or with infants around their skirts. Aggie Turner was in the centre cradling a large bundle close to her chest. The women's voices were hushed, some offered words of comfort, others said nothing; their silence contributing to the increasing air of pessimism.

Unconcerned, a group of children on the village green

played a game of cricket. A spoke from a broken wheel serving adequately as a bat.

With the approach of more than a dozen riders from the direction of Huntingley Manor, the chatter ceased. The men in the duck pond stopped searching. The children forgot their game and ran across the grass to investigate for this group was quite different to the hunt which regularly rode through the village, preceded by a pack of hounds. This time there were no yapping dogs, only a pair of large long-haired Newfoundlands which lolloped along several yards behind the hunters. Despite his lordship riding at the head of the knot, there were no pinks and the bulk of the riders was made up of stable-hands and grooms dressed in their grubby shirts and soiled breeches. Also on this occasion, there was only one lady in the group – though from her riding habit it was hard to differentiate her from the men.

When they stopped on the grass opposite the Spoon and Pudding, there was little conversation and none of the ribald jokes or repartee associated with the hunt, no smiles, laughter, drinks or toasts.

Turning towards the women, Cynthia approached the group and, with a hand prompting her from behind, Aggie Turner stepped forward. The bundle in her arms resembled a pile of dirty laundry tied up in a grey blanket.

Thia nodded. 'Tell me, Aggie, exactly which way did your daughter go?'

'That way, ma'am. Across the field. Over yonder stile. Along by the stream and into the woods. I used to take her that way myself.'

Thia turned to her father. 'We will pick up her trail when we get out of the village.'

Lord Beresford nodded and indicated for one of the stable

lads to take the bundle.

'What is your daughter's name, Aggie?' Thia asked.

'Same as mine, ma'am, but we always call her Agnes.' She hesitated. 'You'll find her, won't you, ma'am?'

'Don't worry, Aggie.' But glancing around the group of villagers, the sombre expressions on their faces were those of a mourning party following a hearse. One wizened old woman shook her head, while another hid her eyes behind the rag she was using as a handkerchief.

'Have faith, Aggie,' Thia called quietly. 'I will find her.'

As the horses walked through the village, a boy's high-pitched voice cried, 'Tally ho!' But the call fell on deaf ears and the riders departed in silence. The group of children ran behind them to the end of the village where the horses broke into a canter and spread out across the field. Increasing their pace to a swinging gallop, they headed towards a low stone wall with a stile set into it. Spurring their mounts, the riders jumped one after the other thudding down into the soft meadow at the other side and surprising the grazing cattle. The horses needed little encouragement. It was a track they had ridden many times before but usually in pursuit of a fox. After splashing along the bank of the stream they reached a hedgerow, and slowed to a stop.

Unassisted, Thia slid from her saddle and called the dogs. Both animals responded immediately, bounding up, tails wagging, happy to receive her attention.

Isaac, the young groom handed Aggie's bundle to her. Untying the bedding, she encouraged the dogs to sniff through the wool and cotton articles.

'Go find!' she instructed, shaking the blanket under the dog's noses as she headed on foot in the direction of the woods.

After zigzagging the grassy path for only a few seconds, the bitch suddenly bristled, then, as if her nose was drawn along the ground by an invisible thread, it headed directly towards the woods. The slightly larger male padded behind his mate, also sweeping the ground for the scent as he ran.

Returning to her mount to murmurs of approval, Thia sensed that the riders' spirits had risen. It was exactly the same feeling as when the hounds took the scent.

After assisting her into the saddle, Isaac rolled up the blanket and remounted. Running ahead, the dogs travelled eagerly, their broad paws silent on the grass, their black coats swaying with each stride like a field of corn in a strong wind. With Lord Beresford and his daughter in the lead, the members of the Huntingley household followed.

Turning in his saddle, Lord Beresford invited the groom to ride alongside him. 'Tell me, Isaac, do you have any idea what the path is like through yonder woods?'

'Aye, my lord. I used to play here when I was a lad.'

'And in your opinion, young man, how far could a youngster stray if she were on her own?'

'Hard to say, sir. I trust not too far. These woods have tracks through them that lead nowhere or go round in circles. Like a maze, it is. Trouble is Henley Woods don't have no end. As you know, my lord, these woods back on to Sherwood Forest and it's real old forest in these parts. You never get riders going in there. It's too dark and overgrown. Besides, there's no deer in these parts to my knowledge.' He paused before continuing, 'If you'll pardon me for saying, sir, but there's plenty of wild boar. Some big ugly beasts roaming these woods. It's no place for anyone alone at night, especially a child.'

Lord Beresford acknowledged the comments and spurred his horse.

As the groom had predicted, it was not long after the riders had entered the woods that the undergrowth thickened and the horses were limited to single file. Undeterred, they walked on, nettles four feet tall fanned their boots while tangled brambles criss-crossing the path, scratched their arms and faces. The thick canopy of summer foliage obliterated the dying sunlight and made the surroundings gloomy. Even from the front of the line, it was impossible to see far ahead. When finally the riders broke through into a glade, everyone was glad to stop. Though the dogs barked and were anxious to go on, most felt it was time to reconsider the situation.

Fully aware that when they had left the village, it was late in the afternoon, Thia had been buoyed by the fact it would not be completely dark for a few hours. But they had been in the saddle for little more than an hour when the degree of darkness in the woods made riding hazardous. Beside that, she was conscious of whisperings exchanged between the older men. Some heads nodded sagely to the suggestion that the search should be abandoned and resumed at dawn.

'Pardon me, your lordship,' one of the men asked politely. 'Is there any hope the little one has survived?'

Lord Beresford looked to his daughter for an answer.

'I shall continue on foot,' she announced boldly, sliding from her mount.

'Cynthia?'

'Don't worry, Papa,' she said, trying to disguise the feelings of frustration in her voice. 'I will be fine. Isaac, tether the horses securely and get the leashes for the dogs. Am I right in thinking that you know these woods?'

'A little, ma'am. I come from round these parts.'

'Then you will accompany me.'

The young man nodded.

31

'And you must return home, Father,' she said softly, as she walked over and stood beside him.

He leaned forward to speak privately. 'Thia, you cannot go alone.'

'I will not be alone. I am taking Isaac, and Byron and Bella. Please do as I say, Father. Go back with the others. I assure you I will be all right. The dogs still have the scent but if it should rain overnight it may be lost by morning.'

The leather creaked as Lord Beresford shifted in his saddle. Looking at the faces around him, he recognized signs of weariness and disappointment. Yet his daughter's face showed none of those features. How well he knew that look of dogged determination which she often wore. How wilful she was, he thought. Just like her mother. He knew that if disparaging remarks were passed about her staying out at night in the company of a young groom, she would care not a jot. It was pointless arguing with her. His daughter was intent on finding the infant and he admired her resolve.

'But what if something should happen?' he added. 'An accident perhaps? Without light you could get hopelessly lost.'

'Nothing will happen, and I have more chance of hearing the girl if we go alone. We have a lamp with us. Isaac will carry that and we will proceed with care. The poor child will think the hounds of hell are after her if she hears a mob of riders approaching.'

Lord Beresford sighed. As usual, she was probably right.

'I will pass word to the village that you are still searching. And I will return to this very spot at first light. I insist Pitkin and Adams stay with your horses and you will send word with one of them should you need any help.'

Thia nodded, her eyes exchanging unspoken words with

her father. He had the utmost faith in his daughter. Taking a silver flask from his pocket, he handed it to her and turned his horse's head.

'Come, Isaac,' Thia said. 'There is no time to waste, and if I'm not mistaken we will lose what little light there is before we can cover much distance.'

'Ready when you are, ma'am.'

Thia watched for a few moments until her father and the rest of the party had left the clearing and the woodland path had closed behind them. It would be almost dark before her father reached Huntingley but ahead darkness was already engulfing the woods.

With the Newfoundlands running ahead, Thia followed the young groom along the narrow path. Every few minutes she called her dogs who returned excitedly, barked and turned, eager to run on. She was confident they were still on the girl's scent.

Cynthia Beresford and the groom made an unlikely pair who spoke little at first. Carrying the lantern in one hand, Isaac apologized each time he inadvertently allowed a branch to swing back into his mistress's face.

Unconcerned, Thia trudged on but after a while she became conscious of her own weariness. Though she rode daily and danced every month, she seldom walked for long distances. Her legs were tired and though the grassy earth was soft underfoot, her feet ached. Despite her discomfort, there was no way she would give in or even admit to the fact.

'When do you expect the moon to rise, Isaac?'

'It'll be awhile before it clears these trees. But if it's like last night, it'll be near full, praise the Lord.'

They walked on, Thia stumbling occasionally on the track

cut by foxes, boars, goats and wild cats. The youth, concerned for her, suggested they rest for a while, but each time Thia declined until they reached a spring which bubbled from some rocks and trickled across their path.

'Just a moment,' she called, stopping and pulling the silver flask from her pocket. The Huntingley crest glinted in the lamplight. 'Do you drink strong liquor, young man?'

'No ma'am. I was given some gin once when I had a tooth pulled. Burned my throat and near choked me. Since then I've had my teeth pulled without it.'

'Then you will not mind if I waste a little,' she said, tipping most of the contents onto the ground and refilling the flask with spring water. 'I should not like to choke young Agnes when we find her.'

'You are confident we will find her, ma'am.'

'Certainly. Aren't you?'

'I hope so, ma'am.'

'Trust the dogs, Isaac. There are no better trackers than the Newfoundlands. I would say their noses are as acute as the hounds'. And far better swimmers too. Bella! Byron!' she called. Within minutes the pair came bounding back, their long hair swinging and tails wagging, competing for her attention.

'Fine animals, ma'am, if I might say. Fine names for the pair of them two.'

Thia smiled. She enjoyed talking about them. 'My great grandfather brought Huntingley's first Newfoundlands from Newstead Abbey. They were descended from the very dog Lord Byron brought from Newfoundland. Have you heard of Lord Byron, the poet?'

When Isaac nodded, Thia wondered if he was only being polite.

'It is a Beresford tradition to remember their background in their names. That is why his lordship's dog has the name Bryon Boatswain Benedict the ninth.'

'That's quite a handle, ma'am, for a pup.'

'Indeed it is,' Thia smiled.

'And what about the other one, Bella? If I might ask?'

'I gave her the name of Lord Byron's wife. I did not think he would mind.' She smiled. 'Twenty years ago, when I was a girl, a new bitch was brought to Huntingley to improve the line. It was all black, like all the previous dogs, but it bore a litter which included some pups daubed with patches of white. Since then every time we have a litter some carry the markings of that bitch. As you can see Bella has those markings.'

'Looks like she stepped in a bucket of white paint, ma'am.'

'Indeed.' Thia laughed. 'Are you familiar with Lord Byron's work?'

'Well, yes and no, ma'am. It's just that when my ma was learning me to read, we only had two books in the house. One was the family Bible of course, and the other was a volume of Lord Byron's poems.'

'How interesting,' said Thia. 'Do you remember the poem he wrote to his dog – Boatswain?'

'Can't say as I do, ma'am. I can remember some of the others though.'

Thia thought for a moment. 'Perhaps the poem I am thinking of was never published in a book. I remember reading it when I visited Newstead Abbey several years ago. It was carved on a tombstone. Boatswain was Lord Byron's favourite dog and he buried him in his garden.'

'Is that the honest truth, ma'am?'

Thia smiled. 'Honest truth,' she repeated, holding up her right hand.

'Well, I'll be. That'll be a tale to tell Ma when I get back – if you don't mind me passing it on, ma'am.'

'You are welcome, Isaac. Now we must rest no longer. Get the dogs back on the scent and lead the way.'

The sounds of night surrounded them. A fox yapped from little more than a stone's throw away. They could both smell it. The haunting hooting of an owl became background noise which Thia soon ignored along with the crackle of branches beneath her feet. In places, thorns and blackberry bushes tore at her breeches and caught on her jacket. She wondered how a child had struggled through the bushes. She was glad to be wearing gloves. The occasional unnerving rustlings in the undergrowth made her mind leap to the boars, but each time Isaac discounted the possibility saying it was only a bird or a squirrel. He assured her that with the dogs running ahead of them the wild pigs wouldn't trouble them. Thia acknowledged his reassurances but didn't know how he could be so sure.

It was becoming damp now and, despite her efforts, her body was feeling chilled. She didn't know how late it was but she knew she was tired. Suddenly, on the path ahead, the dogs let out a peel of barks which were answered by the irate high-pitched snapping of a smaller dog.

'They've found her!' Thia yelled. 'Quickly, Isaac, you can move faster than me.'

The boy stumbled ahead, leaving her in the darkness. Not a flicker of moonlight filtered through the woodland and for a moment she was alone. Then Bella came bounding back, Isaac following.

'She's all right, ma'am!' he shouted. 'Agnes is alive.'

CHAPTER 3

Algernon Beresford

'You're a marvel, ma'am. I've said it before and I'll say it again. God bless you, ma'am.'

Cynthia Beresford appeared not to be listening. Laying her head on the towel resting on the back of the bath-tub, she closed her eyes allowing her tired limbs to absorb the revitalizing warmth of the water.

She could not remember a time when she had been so cold or sore. Yet she had only spent one night in the forest and a summer's night at that, while the child, Agnes, had spent almost two full days and nights in the woods and with little more than her pet dog to keep her warm. How hopelessly vulnerable the child had been.

How relieved she was to have found her.

Ethel Thoroughgood added another handful of perfumed salts to the bath and trickled another jug of warm water over her mistress's shoulders.

'You'll be the talk of the village, how you brought little Agnes out safe. And word'll spread across the country like wild-fire, you mark my words.'

'I truly hope not.' Thia thought about her maid's statement. She had done very little. In her mind, the two dogs were the heroes, and the lad, Isaac. But they would not merit a mention and she would have no control over the local gossip. 'And the news will exasperate my dear brother no end, as he is already extremely peeved at not being involved in the search.'

'But you would have asked Mr Horatio, if he hadn't already been out riding that afternoon.'

'Yes, of course, Goody,' she sighed. 'What troubles me is that if my brother had ridden with us we might never have found young Agnes.'

'Then thank the Lord that you went without him and that you did find her, ma'am.'

'Indeed.' Thia said thoughtfully. 'If Horatio had come he would have taken charge and would have argued against every suggestion I made. Likely he would have probably convinced everyone that such a venture was uncalled for and persuaded dear Papa that we would never find the child – that she was already dead or carried off by some wild animal before we even set off. I would not put it past him to suggest that she had run away from home deliberately, or was hiding and did not want to be found.' She sighed deeply. 'Knowing my brother as I do, if I had suggested we search in one direction, he would have argued that the opposite path was better, and he would never have agreed to take Bella and Byron but would have insisted on riding with hounds. And I pity the poor child if he had stumbled across her. He would have scared the wits out of her. Goodness knows, she was alarmed enough at the sight of Isaac and me.'

Thoroughgood sniffed and wiped the corner of her eye with her index finger. 'One thing's for sure, ma'am, when you have your own children, you'll make a wonderful mother.'

'Enough of that chatter, Goody. Don't you start advising me about marriage. I had quite a dose of that from Horatio only the other day.'

'No, ma'am, I wouldn't dare suggest ... I was only saying. . . .'

Thia turned to her maid and spoke kindly, 'Dear Goody, I understand what you are saying, and you are permitted. Of all people, I think you probably know me better than anyone else.'

Algernon Beresford studied the mosaic of chequered squares inlaid into the polished table. Running his eyes across the ivory pieces which had put paid to his ebony king, he looked puzzled. He had captured more of his opponent's pawns, even taken his queen, yet he had succumbed to the attack so easily.

'I don't believe it,' he said. 'You have done it again, William.'

The expression on his friend's face was apologetic. 'Sorry, Algy, but you did leave yourself wide open.'

Algernon Beresford sighed. 'I'm afraid that is the story of my life.'

'Another game?'

Young Beresford shook his head as he got up and pulled on the tasselled bell-cord beside the fireplace. 'Tea, William?'

'Thank you.'

William Ashley-Parker replaced the pieces on the chess board, while Algernon picked up a wad of handwritten papers from the writing desk. Sinking on to the sofa, he laid the papers on his knee and glanced through the first few sheets. 'Now tell me about your play,' he said. 'I want to hear all about the performance and what the critics had to say. You haven't even told me who played the lead. Has a review appeared in *The Times* yet?'

Looking pensive, William sank into the armchair. His voice was soft. 'I think it went well. The audience seemed to like it. But I do wish you could have been there, Algy. It would have pleased me no end and given me so much more confidence.'

'I don't know why you would need that. Your work is good and always highly acclaimed.'

William lifted a curl which had strayed on to his forehead and laid it back amongst the mop of blond locks which crowned his head.

'I'm afraid in the theatre it's not a case of one's ability.'

'But in your last review—'

'My last review was totally off the point,' William said, shaking his head. 'Reporters are a strange breed. You tell them one thing and they print the contrary. When my previous play premiered, I never mentioned Eton or Cambridge, yet they all centred their articles on my academic background. The fact I made particular mention of my training with the Royal Shakespeare Company never rated a single word.'

'But does it matter what they write providing they are positive?'

'Perhaps not. Just as well a play's success is determined by the audience's reaction on the first night.'

Algernon flipped the pages of the manuscript on his lap. 'How I envy you, William. You are so talented. You write, you paint, you have a fine singing voice and yet you are so modest and are the most inoffensive fellow I know.'

'Next to you, Algy dear.'

The ensuing moment's silence was interrupted by the arrival of the butler announcing that tea was being served, immediately followed by a maid, carrying a large tray decked with china and a plate of sandwiches.

'William!' Thia announced, smiling broadly as she bustled into the room after the servants. 'I didn't realize you were here.'

William rose to his feet and inclined his head and shoulders courteously before greeting Thia with a kiss on her outstretched hand.

Thia pecked him playfully on the cheek. 'May I join you, Algy?' she asked.

'But of course. William was just telling me of his latest success.'

The butler cleared his throat. 'Will you be taking tea, with the gentlemen, ma'am?'

'No, thank you, Jackson.'

Moving further along the sofa, Algernon invited his sister to sit beside him.

'William worked his magic last week at the Grand Theatre in Leeds. He tells me *The Rose Thorn* received a two-minute standing ovation.'

'Bravo!' Thia said, clapping her hands together quietly. 'Oh, I do wish we had been there? Why didn't we go Algy?'

'I promise,' said Algernon, 'when your next play is presented in London, we will all go, won't we, Thia? It's just such a dreadfully long and dreary journey to the north and you know how I hate the train.'

'Ah!' Thia heaved a long disappointed breath, the lines of dejection furrowing her face. 'Sorry, William,' she said. 'It is not your theatre production which I am sighing about. It's just that I came to ask Algy a question and it concerns travel-ling.'

Algernon Beresford curled up his nose. 'To the north, you

41

mean? Not Scotland, I hope?'

'Sorry, Brother, the wrong direction. South and west – a long way south and west.'

'Let me guess, Portsmouth? Exeter? Torquay? I don't object to Torquay. It is quite a pleasant resort.'

Thia shook her head but was unable to hide a coy grin – like that of a child about to offer a Christmas gift to a favourite aunt or reveal a long-held secret. 'A little further than that,' she said, prolonging the anticipation. 'Patagonia!'

'South America!' Algernon blurted, dumbfounded.

Unperturbed, Thia continued, 'Papa agrees it will be a wonderful place to visit. What an adventure it will be: crossing the Atlantic on a sailing ship, riding across the pampas, climbing the Andes, sailing through the Magellan Strait, following in the wake of the *Beagle*, and standing on the very end of the earth's tail.'

Algernon swallowed hard and looked beseechingly at his friend. But William's eyes were alight with excitement.

'What a venture!' William said.

'You really think so?'

'Of course, Algy. Imagine the dialogue written into the landscape – the wild seas, the mountains, the plains, the diversity of scenery, the people. What pictures I could paint in oils or narrative. What a story such a journey would tell!'

'Are you saying that Papa has agreed to go?' Algy asked.

'Yes,' said Thia, 'and he is looking forward to it.'

Algy looked to his friend. 'Would you consider going along with us, William?'

'I would go tomorrow, if I were invited.'

'Of course you are invited,' said Thia. 'Then that is all settled.'

'Wait a moment,' Algy said drily.

Although enthusiasm fired Thia to continue, she recognized the firm yet kindly tone in her brother's voice and withheld her next comment. Her twin brother had always been more prudent than she though she constantly accused him of being overcautious. But besides being less impulsive, he was always careful, considerate and thoughtful. Algernon Beresford possessed more of their father's nature and character traits than Thia did and she envied him a little for that. As they had grown and matured, she had learned to accept his habit of pondering over proposals, and of never rushing into decisions irrespective of whether they were important or insignificant.

Thia tucked her legs underneath herself while William drew up a straight chair and sat down opposite the pair.

'First of all,' Algernon asked, 'tell me who is going on this expedition?'

'Papa and you and I, and now William too, and naturally we will take two or three of the servants. And I shall take Bella and Byron of course.' She looked first to her brother's friend, a man slightly younger than herself, whose recalcitrant curls continued to creep back on to his forehead, then to her brother. 'Say you will come, Algy. Please say you will.'

'But what about Horatio? You didn't include him.'

'Horatio will stay and be master of Huntingley for the six months we are away.'

'I am sure he will revel in that,' Algy replied, a hint of cynicism in is voice. 'I hope you have asked him.'

'All in good time, Algy. Do say you will come.'

William leaned forward and looked eagerly at his friend. 'Say yes, Algy, and on the ship, I promise I will teach you the secrets of winning at chess.'

'But I know nothing about this far-away place you are

planning to descend upon.'

'So much the better, we will enjoy the experience of discovering it together.'

Thia and William exchanged eager glances while they waited for a response. But before answering, Algernon's eyes and mouth contorted spontaneously as the undesirable aspects of the forthcoming journey flashed through his head. He looked questioningly at his sister and his best friend as though the pair were recommending he underwent a surgical procedure with no form of anaesthetic. Eventually, after what seemed like several minutes, his pained expression disappeared and a broad smile mellowed his face.

'If I must come with you, then I suppose I must,' he said. 'But tell me, Thia, when is this venture gong to take place?'

'Just as soon as a passage can be arranged. Papa has business in London next week and I intend to accompany him. We will visit the offices of one of the shipping companies and book berths on a steamer. It is important we depart as soon as possible as we must arrive before Christmas which is summer in the southern hemisphere. It would be foolhardy to travel there in their winter season.'

Algernon turned to his friend. 'I must learn more about this wild land my dear sister is intent on subjecting us to. And in the meantime, William, you can start planning your next play about some aspect of our travels.'

A broad grin creased the corners of Thia's eyes, as she leaned over and hugged her twin brother. 'Wonderful, Algy. I knew you would agree.'

'Thia...!' he called, but she had already bounced up and did not stop to listen. Her silk skirt rustled against the door as she hurried out.

'Come, William,' Algernon said. 'Let us repair to the library.

You can read to me about Patagonia – this God-forsaken place at the bottom of the world.'

'Excuse me, ma'am, sorry for interrupting, but young Jimmy Turner, one of the stable lads, asked me if I could hand this to you personally.' Ethel Thoroughgood held out her hand. In it was a small package wrapped in a sheet of crumpled paper.

Thia looked at her maid quizzically as she opened it.

'It'll be from Aggie, ma'am.'

Inside the package was a large white cotton handkerchief neatly folded three times. Thia examined it closely turning it from one side to the other.

'Look, Goody,' she said, pointing to the initials CB embroidered in coloured silk in two of the corners and the border of pink flowers which ran around the edge. 'See how neat her stitches are.'

'It's very nice, ma'am. Shame she couldn't give you something more proper – with lace, I mean. But I imagine she'd not have the money to afford it.'

'Don't apologize for her, Goody. It is a fine kerchief and her fancy work is admirable. She obviously has far more patience than I. Please give my thanks to the boy to convey to Aggie. Tell her that I shall take it with me when we go away. Oh! That reminds me,' she said, 'you must start making preparations for our holiday.'

Ethel cocked her head. 'Holiday, ma'am? Where to?'

'Oh! I am sorry, I haven't had chance to mention it yet as it has only just been arranged. We are going to Patagonia.'

'Pat-a-what, ma'am?'

'Patagonia, South America. We shall be away for at least six months. It may be hot on the journey and when we arrive it will be warm. But it could also be quite cold in some places as there is snow in the mountains. I will need dresses for dinner on the ship but casual clothes and trousers to wear when we are travelling through the countryside. We are all going, Goody. Algy and I, and Papa. Of course, Mr Horatio will stay at Huntingley, which reminds me I must speak with him about it. Aren't you excited, Goody?'

'Yes, ma'am,' her maid said, tentatively.

'And you will need a riding habit as much of the overland journey will be on horseback. Perhaps an old one of mine could be made to fit.'

Ethel Thoroughgood's jaw dropped. 'Did I hear you right, ma'am? Riding clothes? You mean, me riding on a horse?'

'That's right, Goody. You can ride, can't you?'

'Not likely, ma'am. You wouldn't catch me anywhere near one of them great big sweaty things.' Shaking her head, she continued, 'And you certainly won't get me on the back of one of 'em!'

'Well, I won't go without you and I don't intend taking any of the other maids. There is only one thing for it. You must take lessons. Leave it to me, we have the time. I will arrange for Arkwright to give you some instruction.'

'Oh, no, ma'am. Definitely not Mr Arkwright! If I really have to learn – not that I want to – then let it be anyone but Edmund Arkwright.'

'And what is it about Mr Arkwright you dislike so much?'

Ethel thought carefully for a moment before answering. 'Nothing really, ma'am. It's just his attitude. When he's in the stables, he behaves like he's master of the manor, if you'll pardon me for saying. And besides that, him and me don't get on.'

Thia looked surprised.

'Leave it to me, Goody. I know one of the young grooms

who I am sure will make an excellent teacher. And if the weather is fine tomorrow, you shall take your first riding lesson.'

Sitting aside with her legs hooked over the saddle's horns, Ethel tried to sit upright, but, as she straightened her back, she felt that at any moment she would lose her balance, slide off the highly polished seat and topple headlong on to the cobbled courtyard.

'Just relax,' Isaac said, at the same time encouraging the horse to remain still.

'I'm trying,' she said, 'but it's not easy.'

As she spoke Edmund Arkwright emerged from one of the stalls. He stood for a while watching her, tapping the tip of his riding crop on the side of his boots. Not wanting their eyes to meet, Ethel gripped the reins and stared straight ahead as the youth walked the mare slowly around the courtyard. As they passed Arkwright, she heard the slap of a hand on the horse's rump. Her mount jerked forward, sending her reeling in the saddle like a Saturday drunk. Grabbing a handful of mane in both hands, she held on tightly and prayed that she would not fall off.

'Whoa!' Isaac cried, as he restrained the mare and calmed her. 'Are you all right, Mrs Thoroughgood?'

Ethel nodded. She was nervous and angry. Arkwright's actions hadn't surprised her. His spiteful nature was not new. She'd heard stories about the man – whispered tales which had carried from the stable yard to the scullery, even above stairs and though she usually tried to stay clear of such gossip, word ran through the house quicker than fire up a curtain. She knew full well many of the murmurings were not just mere tittle-tattle.

Uppermost in her mind was an incident she could never forget: the day Arkwright dismissed one of the stable lads for stealing. Ethel had known the lad since he was an infant and watched him grow into a kind, God-fearing lad who never had a bad word for anyone. She'd even put in a good word for him with his lordship for him to get the job at Huntingley. When the accusations were first laid it came as a shock to everyone. No one believed the boy was a thief and the lad's mother swore it was not true. She found it hard enough to bear the brunt of the charges against her son. But the shame of his dismissal was even worse and when her son's body was found hanging from the bough of an old oak, it broke his mother's heart. Everyone knew that the items, which Arkwright accused the boy of taking, would never be found. And they never were. But after a while folk stopped talking about it and the matter was forgotten. But Ethel swore at the time she would never forget. How could she – the lad was her nephew?

Though she couldn't see Arkwright's face as he walked across the courtyard, Ethel could imagine the satisfied sneer lingering on his lips. His actions had come as no surprise, in fact she should have expected something like that to happen. She was grateful her mistress had arranged for Isaac to give her the lessons and not Arkwright, and thankful the head groom's actions hadn't resulted in her being dislodged from the saddle and falling. It looked a long way down. Promising herself that she would say nothing to her mistress, Ethel was determined to master the skill and over the next six weeks would arrange her instruction at a time when Edmund Arkwright was occupied elsewhere.

Taking a deep breath and concentrating hard, she straightened her back and for a moment felt a tinge of pride sitting high above the cobbles. But being led around the courtyard was one thing and riding across the open pampas, whatever that was, was an entirely different matter. But she intended to persevere looking forward to the Beresford family's vacation, knowing full well that the head groom was not included in the party embarking on the voyage to the nether regions of the world.

CHAPTER 4

Liverpool Docks

Algernon Beresford looked north from the Coburg Dock and shook his head. 'I can honestly say, I have never seen such a place!'

'Indeed, it is wonderful, isn't it? So vibrant and full of colour!'

Algy turned and looked blankly at his friend, before casting his eyes from the expanse of the River Mersey to the patchwork of docks abutting the busy city of Liverpool. 'My dear fellow, you must be jesting!' he said. 'Look around. There is not a hint of green to be seen anywhere and I doubt if there is a blade of grass growing within ten miles of this God-forsaken place. The river is the colour of mud and the sky the colour of lead. Even the woeful creatures who frequent this area are daubed with the grime of yonder chimneys.' His eyes flitted along the docks to the line of coal wagons, the cranes and hoists and steam engines. 'The sounds jar the eardrums, the smells offend the nostrils and some of the sights I find myself closing my eyes to. As to colour; the only hint of red is the fire in the forge over yonder and that only glows when the bellows breathe life into it. My dear William, in all honesty, tell me you are joking. I cannot imagine a place more devoid of colour.'

'I am talking metaphorically, Algy dear. I am not looking merely at a palette of colours. I am looking at life, at movement, at noise. The cacophony of voices, the variety of shapes, the classes of ships, the expressions on the faces. Don't you see them? Compare the bold warehouses with the assortment of church spires. Look at the elegant domes and cupolas. Such a remarkable skyline. You must look at the picture as a whole. Consider the people on the dock. See how different they are. The way they dress. The baggage they carry. Each is unique. Yet when you step back and view the scene as a whole, they intermesh as neatly as pieces of a jigsaw puzzle – hundreds of tiny cameos yet all complimentary, each one adding to the composition. He smiled sympathetically at his companion. Remind me to teach you to see things the way I see them, Algy. You must learn to open your mind not just your eyes, and to give rein to your imagination. I fear you are missing so much. Everything is so vibrant, so alive, so rich in . . . colour.'

'Dear William, I believe I shall need more than lessons in the game of chess while we are aboard. But I doubt, even if we travelled ten times around the globe, I could ever learn to interpret things the way you do. How I envy you my friend.'

'Come, Algy.'

As they strolled along the dockside, a carriage, drawn by a pair of fine greys, rolled along the road, passing within a few yards of them. The friends stopped and watched as it finally creaked to a halt near the forward gangway of the packet steamer.

'Steady!' the driver called, his voice just audible at that

distance. The man sitting on the seat beside him slipped a fur cloak from his shoulders, placed it over his arm and swung down.

William touched Algernon's arm. 'Let us observe for a moment.'

'Observe what?'

'That fellow who has just alighted. There is something decidedly unusual about him.'

'Then let us go and introduce ourselves.'

'Not at this point, my friend. Based only on intuition, I believe a discreet distance is preferable at the present.'

Algernon shrugged his shoulders. He was familiar with the odd whims of his companion. Dutifully he watched as the man rolled the garment neatly before handing it to a waiting porter. Even on the dock, surrounded by a motley mob of steerage passengers, the stranger looked out of place. His shirt was partly open and he had a large kerchief tied around his neck. He wore no coat and his waistcoat was buttoned only halfway. His trousers, which showed signs of wear at the knees, were tucked into a pair of well-worn boots. The dark leather was decorated with embossed carvings which ran around the top.

'What do you make of him, Algy?'

'A foreigner, I would say. Not long returned from abroad.'

'And what brings you to that conclusion?'

'Apart from the fur, his skin is the colour of Jackson's afternoon brew.'

'Well done, my friend. You are improving. I admit his footwear appears exotic although I would argue that he is probably English as his facial features reveal nothing of foreign blood.'

'But what of that moustache – unkempt, untrimmed,

ungentlemanly. And his hair, long and plaited in a queue, as worn by a common sailor. Then there is the Basque style of beret he is wearing. Definitely a foreigner. An adventurer maybe. Travelling alone it seems. And most undoubtedly carrying a third-class ticket.'

'You make that judgement from his outward appearance.'

'Naturally. How else can I make an assessment?'

'But what of the colour of his hair? It is light brown, is it not? While his moustache has a tinge of ginger about it. Also, his eyes are blue and the lines radiating across his temples indicate he has spent much time squinting in bright sunlight.'

'Now I know you are jesting. You cannot possibly see those details from this distance.'

William smiled cheekily. 'I admit to cheating a little. I took note of his face when the carriage drove past us. It was those features which sparked my interest in him.'

'Well, I still contend he's a foreigner. Russian perhaps, or an Austrian, though the plaited hair and the black beret puzzle me. As for the broad belt, I've never seen anything quite like that before. If I'm not mistaken it's inlaid with pieces of silver. Perhaps he is Spanish or Portuguese. And by the evil look of that curved scabbard lodged under his belt, the fellow would make a fine antagonist in one of your plays.'

William Ashley-Parker smiled at his friend. 'I'm afraid if I presented such a character on the London stage the audience would laugh and say such people did not exist. But I will make you a wager, Algy. Five pounds says that before we cross the Equator, I will have sketched a portrait of him. With such a striking face and such a strange intense expression, I shall seek him out and persuade him to sit for me.'

'So be it,' Algy said.

No sooner than the bet was agreed upon than the stranger

stared in their direction. Despite the distance between them, the man's timing and expression seemed to indicate that he was privy to their conversation. Then he looked away.

'He knows we were watching him,' William said. 'Can't you read it in his expression?'

Algernon shook his head. 'He hardly glanced our way and there are plenty of other people on the dock. Why would he be interested in us?'

'I think the reverse applies. It is we who are interested in him and I believe it is that fact which concerns him.'

'Ah,' said the young aristocrat flippantly. 'I see I shall also need lessons in mind reading.'

'Such an intriguing face,' William said.

'Colourful!' Algy added, with a wry smile.

From the floor of the carriage, the driver retrieved a carpet bag, a portmanteau and a saddle and handed them to two stewards who took them straight on board the ship. From the seat the man collected two rifles which he rested into the crook of his arm.

'A foreign general, perhaps?'

'A mercenary, I would suggest, Algy.'

After settling his dues with the coach driver, the stranger threw a coarse woven blanket over his left shoulder, turned and strode across the dock to the steamer. Showing no interest in the hub of activity going on around, the newly arrived passenger was greeted with a degree of polite, but cordial familiarity by one of the ship's young officers. As he crossed the gangway he stopped for a moment to cast a look in the direction of the two well-dressed gentlemen.

'So why does he not have to go though all those awful formalities and inspections we were confronted with?' Algy asked.

'Perhaps he boarded earlier as we did and his luggage was delayed. Such things happen you know.'

'An offensive fellow to my mind. Probably does not even speak English. I am thankful he will not be sharing our saloon.'

Deep in his own thoughts, William was oblivious to his friend's opinion. 'We must find out more about him when we are at sea. A few discreet enquiries to the purser should do the trick, but as he is boarding at the forward end, one can only assume he holds a first-class ticket. If that is the case, you must invite him to dine with us.'

'Well, if you insist.'

'I do indeed. Come, Algy,' William said, taking his friend by the arm. 'Let us return on board and see if the stewards have finished unpacking our trunks. And we must find out what mischief Cynthia is up to. I wouldn't be surprised if she already knows the total geography of the ship and the names and ranks of all its officers. And, no doubt, by the time your father arrives tomorrow she will be familiar with the status of every first-class passenger too, including where they hail from, their port of disembarkation and the purpose of their journey.'

'William, if I did not know you better, I would say there was a degree of cynicism in your tone.'

'Thank you for qualifying your comment, Algy. I could never speak disparagingly of Thia. Your sister is the most exciting woman I have ever met. She is intelligent, bold and as outspoken as any man I know, and I admire her immensely. I only wish I had her confidence.'

Algernon looked at his friend and smiled. 'You have courage and confidence in sufficient quantities for both of us, William. Come, let us go find this sister of mine.'

'Goodness gracious, ma'am, I don't know how you'll manage in here. It's no bigger than a broom closet. And the bed, it's as hard as a board and the mattress no thicker than a blanket. I'd heard these modem liners were like floating palaces.'

'Indeed, the latest ships from the Cunard and White Star Line are, but unfortunately they don't sail to the port we are going to. The Pacific Steam Navigation Company's mail packets are the only ones which sail from here to Valparaiso and stop at Punta Arenas in Strait of Magellan.'

'Goodness, ma'am, it all sounds like a foreign language to me.'

'Never mind, Goody. The main thing is that we get there safely. As to the accommodation, it suits me admirably and if the bed is hard then I will not be in danger of sleeping too long. I trust you are satisfied with your cabin.'

'Oh, yes, thank you, ma'am. It's mighty fine. Nicely fitted out, though I doubt I'll spend much time in there. It ain't got one of those round windows, so I'll have to keep a lamp burning all the time, or I'll never find my way out.'

Thia grinned. 'And what about young Isaac? He looked a little bewildered when we came aboard.'

'He'll be all right, ma'am. Last time I saw him, he was all excited about having a bunk to himself. Says they are stacked three tiers high and he's got to share a cabin with a dozen other men, but he don't mind. Says it's a real adventure for him. Never imagined he'd ever have chance to do anything like this in his lifetime.'

Thia trailed her finger across the condensation on the glass window. 'I wish Lord Beresford had come up to Liverpool with us last week. I just cannot imagine what has delayed him. It's so unlike him. He usually loves to be onboard early. He takes great pleasure in familiarizing himself with the ship before it leaves.'

'And when will that be, ma'am?'

'Tomorrow evening. On the high tide. I fear if he does not board by noon the ship will sail without him.'

'Then I pray they don't meet with any mishaps on the way.'

'I shall not even consider that prospect.'

The Pacific Steam Navigation Company's mail packet was not a modern steamer, in fact she was an old and tired iron ship which many years earlier had been superseded on the Atlantic run by faster, larger and more luxurious vessels. Unable to compete, she had found service on a voyage which few other ships wanted to embark on – carrying mail from England to the west cost of South America.

Five years earlier, in 1880, she had been completely refurbished to accommodate 600 third-class passengers in reasonable comfort, but because of its primary function as a cargo carrier, there was little space for first-class staterooms or sumptuous saloons. The eighteen passenger cabins were small and the first-class passengers had to share the dining facilities with the captain and his crew. Those cabins were located amidships slightly forward of the two funnels.

At 400 feet long and weighing 4,500 tons she was a solid ship and when fully laden was reputed to average sixteen knots.

With its power coming from its single screw propeller rather than wind, the steam packet was guaranteed not to suffer the fate meted out in the Doldrums to sailing ships. Passengers could be assured that they would arrive in Punta Arenas within a day or two of the estimated date of arrival which was mid-November.

*

Morning mist hung over the river and wharfs but the gloom did not deter the early risers – the vagrants who made the docks their home. Emerging from the empty wagons, draughty corners or the doorways of the bond store, they crawled from their nooks like hungry rats. The chance of begging a shilling to buy their next bottle, was their only thought.

To the north, the bell in the Victoria Tower announced the tide was at its lowest ebb. Fog horns wailed on the half empty river as local boats and barges bravely navigated the foggy waterway. But as the fog started to lift and a pale hazy sun filtered through, carts and conveyances of all descriptions began appearing, vying for space on the dockside already occupied by the molehills of human dunnage. Porters, stevedores, ship's stewards and customs officials fussed about like women, arguing over the right to process the rapidly increasing throng of steerage passengers, mostly emigrants, who were congregating around the gangways impatient to get on board. After hours of frustration, some set out their own tables and chairs, even warmed soup on open fires lit on the wharf ignoring the threats of prosecution from the superintendent of the wharf.

A handful of first-class passengers who had boarded the previous day ventured on deck early. Woken by the unfamiliar noises they strolled arrogantly along their allocated section of the decking, stopping at times to lean over the rail, observe, point and laugh in an exaggerated fashion, indulging themselves in a feeling of ultimate superiority.

As the day progressed, the dampness returned. The rain was

invisible. The drizzle so fine it failed to form drops of water, yet it had a palpable wetness about it. The expression on the face of the early morning flower seller reflected the droop of yesterday's blooms as she found no buyers for her posies.

With the bunkering complete, the last of the coal wagons rolled off the wharf as the final deliveries of fresh produce – bread, hogs heads, hams, even a live cow – were boarded amidships.

By this time, the ship itself had come alive. With half its boilers lit the steam packet hummed, its pulse vibrating through every bulwark, rail and metal fitting.

Despite the fact the passengers were allowed to board twenty-four hours before sailing, the majority had only arrived that morning. The Irish ferry had been delayed by bad weather, not arriving until after midnight. Unable to board the mail packet at that hour, the steerage passengers had been forced to wait on the dockside until they could be processed. The unruly queue which hardly seemed to move appeared to be made up mostly of women, though perhaps it was the children's cries which made their presence more evident than the men. Everyone, save for the smallest, was laden with bags or bedding, food for the voyage or cooking pots and pans.

Between the dock and the ship, the wooden gangway bounced beneath the straggle of human cargo. Most appeared anxious as they walked across, hardly daring to glance down to the rising waters of the Mersey River beneath them. The relief and excitement, which had been shared when they arrived at the port, had fizzled. The smiles were gone. The sullen expressions were a product of being made to wait for hours without food or adequate shelter. That only added to the weariness of the journey to Liverpool which had begun several days earlier.

Men cursed; women cried, as they pushed their children along the gangway to the opening in the ship's side. For most this was the ultimate bridge from which there was no turning back. The dark gaping hole which consumed each family group was the gateway to their destiny. The officer at the hatch represented a white-clad St Peter to the Irish emigrants, directing them which way to go. But whatever fate awaited them, the final reckoning would be far from England's shores.

'Do you think they will find their Utopia, Goody?' Thia said, observing from the ship's rail.

'And what would that be, ma'am?'

'The promised land. A fortune in gold maybe. An escape from the meagre existence they have known. The chance of a new life in South America.'

'Strikes me, ma'am, working-class folk will never be no better off no matter where they go. They'll have to work for a living and they'll always bear the mark of where they came from – if you know what I mean.'

Thia watched the line feeding into the hull while her maid was more interested in the hoard of emigrants still waiting to be processed.

'I hope there'll not be taking all those poor folk. The ship's bound to sink if they do.'

Around three o'clock the sound of chatter and the clatter of wagon wheels ceased. Only one of the gangways remained in operation. Seamen appeared from within the ship to make preliminary preparation for unmooring the steamer and taking her to sea. On the dock, the atmosphere took on a different air. From the disorganized unruly chaos seen earlier arose a business-like urgency. While the neatly uniformed stewards had attended to the passengers with polite gestures, tipping their caps and bowing where appropriate, the seamen went about their work in silence, scowling at anyone who got in their way.

Coming out on deck for the umpteenth time, Thia and her maid witnessed the hugs and kisses exchanged between brokenhearted relatives who had said their last tearful farewells, knowing they would never see each other again.

The rope barrier running the length of the dock which had held back the boisterous crowd and separated them from the more affluent passengers now barred only a smattering of spectators, well-wishers and friends who had remained to wave their hats or handkerchiefs to the packet when it was towed out on to the river.

A noisy carriage rumbled along the dock. It was being driven at a speed far faster then was practical or safe. Its arrival caused some family groups to scatter and brought with it a tirade of shouts and cries which attracted everyone's attention.

'Out of the way!' a porter shouted, attempting to clear a path.

'They're here, ma'am!' Ethel cried excitedly.

'At last,' said Thia. It was definitely the Huntingley carriage stacked with luggage on the roof.

When it came to a halt, the driver swung down, dusted his coat and quickly instructed two porters to offload the luggage from the roof. Stepping to the door, he stood straight and rapped a cane across the side of his boot. The gesture was unmistakable.

Ethel Thoroughgood caught her breath.

'What is it, Goody?'

'It's him, ma'am. Edmund Arkwright. What on earth is he doing here? Surely he's not going with us. This is terrible.'

Thia ignored her maid's remarks. She was not interested in the groom, though she watched him lower the carriage's foot-step and open the door. Her eyes widened as the passenger stepped down. It was her brother. Casting his eyes over the steamship, Horatio Beresford stepped down and, from his demeanour, it was obvious that he was not impressed.

'What has happened to Papa?' Thia breathed. 'And where are my dogs? We can't sail without them. I must go down to the wharf and find out what has gone wrong.'

Pushing her way rudely past the officer standing in the hatch-way, Thia ran down the gangway and across the dockside to the carriage, her head spinning.

'What are you doing here?' she cried, to her brother.

'That is a fine welcome,' said Horatio, kissing his sister on the cheek.

'I'm sorry, Horatio, but this is not what I planned. I expected Father. Where is he?'

As she spoke the two Newfoundlands jumped down from the carriage to greet her, almost knocking her from her feet.

'Here I am,' Lord Beresford called, from within. 'Damn gout meant I could hardly walk for a week so Horatio graciously volunteered to accompany me to make sure I arrived safely.'

Thia's eyes followed her brother as he went off to attend to his father's ticket.

'Don't worry,' Lord Beresford said, in her ear. 'Horatio isn't sailing with us.'

For once Thia felt terribly guilty. In retrospect it had been wrong of her not to invite him to travel with them. But she was pleased he had come to see them off.

'I thought Jackson was coming with you, Papa?'

'I think he may be needed at Huntingley, and besides Horatio tells me there are plenty of young stewardesses on the steamer so there will be no call for a butler.'

'Dear Papa,' Thia said, kissing him.

'As to the riding and sleeping under the stars, Horatio is concerned not only for my welfare, but also for Algernon's.'

'Algy will cope just fine. He will have William and me with him. Besides, I am sure he will prove himself to be surprisingly adaptable.'

Though she didn't comment, she commended her brother's concern for her twin. It was the first time she had ever heard him express such a heartfelt feeling.

After passing a few disparaging remarks about the size and age of the ship, Horatio declined his sister's invitation to go aboard and did not linger. As soon as Lord Beresford and his luggage had been conveyed aboard, it was time to say good-bye.

The embrace was brief but it was given in a warmer manner than Thia could ever remember experiencing from her brother before.

'Take good care of Papa,' Horatio said. 'And don't get eaten. It would be such a shame to see your new riding habits torn to shreds.'

Turning, Horatio Beresford climbed into his carriage. 'Home, Arkwright,' he called, tapping his hand on the carriage wall.

Standing alone, Thia waited for him to wave, but he did not look around.

CHAPTER 5

Crossing the Atlantic

The second night aboard, the sea heaved. The steam packet pitched and waves crashed across the bow sending slurries of spume and froth washing across the deck and spewing from the forward scuppers. Instead of cutting through the Atlantic swell the steamer hit it head on, pitching forward and back – the resounding thwack reverberating throughout the length of the whole ship.

'If you'll take my advice, ma'am, viewing the sea from the port side would be preferable.'

Gripping the rail, Thia lifted her head an inch from her hands, turned her head slightly then returned her face to the direction of the water. Apart from feeling dreadful, she was angry, frustrated and vulnerable. This was not what she had anticipated of the holiday. She had sailed to the Continent several times before but never experienced such seas or suffered in this manner. With the frustrations she had experienced on the dock at Liverpool, her guilt at the way she had treated her brother, her father's incapacity, and now this, she wished she had never planned the venture or stepped foot on the mail boat. She had already resolved in her mind to disembark when the ship reached Madeira.

'I would suggest the port side,' the voice repeated. Though more emphatic, the voice was soft and carried on it the slight lilt of a Welsh accent.

'Go away!' she called, not even raising her head. She had no idea who was speaking to her from the darkness and presumed it was a steward. Who else but a fool or a dying man would be out on deck in this weather? Perhaps that was why he did not show himself. Didn't he realize she was ill? She was not leaning over the rail watching the sea race by because she wanted to. Besides which there was nothing to see. Beneath her was nothing but blackness which slid by continually. If she looked up, the sky was the same colour, only that did not move. 'Go away!' she yelled again. 'I am not interested in a view. Can't you see I'm sick?'

The speaker, merely a dark shadow on the poorly illuminated deck, did not move.

'I could walk you to the port side, or I can call someone to attend you.'

Thia breathed deeply and was about to reply, but instead of words her stomach heaved on its emptiness renting the last spoonful of bilious green fluid from the depths of her stomach projecting it out towards the sea. But with the wind blowing towards her, it was immediately returned.

'Ugh!' she sighed, as unsolicited tears welled into her eyes and she grabbed her handkerchief to wipe the vile liquid from her face.

Unable to speak, she inclined her head. Now she realized

what the man had been trying to tell her. Why had she been so stupid?

From the corner of her eye, she made out the outline of a man. The tip of his cigar burned red for a moment as the fire consumed the dead leaves. She couldn't see the smoke breathe from his mouth, but she could smell it. It reminded her of Huntingley.

'No ship has yet been built to challenge the sea. To sail on it, yes. But to meet it head on and receive its full force in the bow – I don't think so. Converting sailing ships to steam, emasculates the ship. Renders it lifeless. Leaves its hull sitting upright on the water like a hare waiting to be shot.'

Thia had no interest in the man's opinions on sailing ships, or steam power, or hares. She could think of nothing more demeaning than being seen in her present condition, but in her current state of mind most thoughts of decorum had left her.

'As to the amount of coal ships like this consume, I can say with certainty it is like a thirsty man consumes water. Where I was born, men now tunnel like moles in the ground to satisfy the needs of industry.'

'No doubt you would prefer to dig gold from the ground to further your fortune?' she breathed cynically, not releasing her grip.

There was no reply. Was he still there? His silence now angered her. If he must bother her with his inconsequential conversation then at least he should reply to her enquiry.

After a while he spoke. 'Gold only brings ill fortune. Chasing it is a fool's errand especially from the shifting sands of the sea.'

Attempting to stand upright, she wiped her chin with her handkerchief while clinging tightly to the rail with the other hand. The idea of sifting gold from the sea sounded ludicrous. She wondered what manner of man was addressing her.

'Excuse me, sir, but I believe we have not been properly introduced.'

'Of course, English tradition must be maintained at all cost.' He stepped forward into the light, inclined his head and introduced himself. 'Euan Davies *en route* to South America,' he said, before stepping back into the shadow. He was not a steward or seaman but the stranger who she had seen boarding at the docks. As he appeared to be wearing the same clothing, perhaps that was the reason he did not dine with the other first-class passengers, she thought.

Thia attempted to look relaxed but her diaphragm locked like an iron vice and the desire to vomit sent her reeling back to the rail. She wanted to introduce herself but dared not open her mouth for the fear of losing more of her stomach's content.

'Two days and you will be completely well. *Mal de mer* doesn't last long. Drink water and eat a dish of dried oatmeal. Now if you will excuse me, I wish you good night.'

Before Thia was able to respond, the man disappeared from the empty deck, its only light spilling from several of the cabin windows. The oil lamps, hanging along the deck at irregular intervals, offered little light.

She shivered. The night wind from the north was cold. And it was wet with spray blown from the bow as it sliced headlong into the waves. She was aware she couldn't stay there all night but to be confined in the cabin would only make her sickness worse. Now her whole body was beginning to shake and she was feeling very weary. Sliding down to the deck she lifted her knees and laid her head on them. Despite the thumping of the engines hammering in her ears, the vibrations rumbling through the ship, the smoke from funnel as the wind veered around, the smell of burning mineral oil and the stench of human cargo swept up from the ventilation shafts, she was unable to induce herself to move. She prayed for sleep.

'Are you all right, miss?'

Thia opened her eyes and leaned her head back. From the outline of his hat Thia recognized the man as one of the stewards.

'I'll get someone to attend to you right away, miss.'

She did not want to be seen in this situation. People could think she was drunk. She attempted to pull herself to her feet again but as soon as she moved her head, the deck around her began to move. She was slowly sliding sideways.

'Thia.' It was the gentle voice of her brother, Algy. Taking her arm, he helped her up. 'So,' he said playfully, 'this is the adventure which you were so eager to embark on. Not quite the gentle carriage ride you had imagined. You there,' he called, to one of the stewards. 'Go fetch the lady's maid. Tell her to come quickly.'

Thia heard the sound of feet running on the decking. She could smell the brandy and cigars her brother had obviously left to walk out on the deck. She could feel his face leaning over hers. Hear his words whispered directly into her ear. 'Don't let the other passengers see you like this, Thia. It is most unbecoming and certainly not your style.'

Algy was right. He usually was. But with her mind as parched as her throat, she was unable to answer. But there was something about her brother's words which were unusual. She had never heard that tone before and she knew instantly he was not berating her for her unladylike behaviour, but he was encouraging her to be strong. What a strange reversal of roles, if only for a few brief moments.

'Take my arm,' he said kindly.

Thia leaned against him as the deck swayed and her head swam on her shoulders.

'Now walk with me, Thia.' His voice was soft but officious and Thia did not argue but allowed him to lead her to her cabin.

Through the portside windows of the first-class passengers' dining-room the panorama of Funchal Bay was visible, the town built around the old fort and battlements.

An hour later the steam packet was unloading mail on the wharf at Funchal. From the deck the passengers watched a larger and more elegant Cunard liner sail from the harbour on its voyage to New York.

'The marvel of steam power!' William said. 'What an exciting era we live in. Don't you agree, Algy?'

Algernon was more interested in the pair of kippers on his plate than the activities on the dock. When the last of the salty fish was stripped from the bone, he wiped his lips with his napkin, then folded it neatly and returned it to the table. 'I agree, William. Whatever you say.'

As Cynthia entered the breakfast-room, the two men stood up.

'Good morning, Thia. I hope you are feeling better. We have missed you these last two days.'

'I am absolutely fine, thank you, William. It must have been something I ate which disagreed with me because suddenly I never felt better.'

'Then we will not be aborting the journey and disembarking here?'

'Goodness, William, you didn't take that proposition

69

seriously, did you?'

Algernon looked across at his friend and winked. 'During the course of this voyage, I will give you instruction on understanding the fickleness of a woman's logic, William. Especially that of my dear sister. She is a complete mystery at times.'

William smiled. 'I believe we will all learn something from travelling together.'

'We certainly will,' Thia said jauntily, after dropping a kiss on her brother's head. 'After breakfast you must tell me about everything I have missed. I want to know precisely who is who and what you have discovered about them. And after that I would like to read to you and Papa a little of Mr Darwin's description of the tail end of the world. Tierra del Fuego is a truly fascinating place which we must visit while we are in the region.'

William smiled, but though Thia did not notice, his expression was tinged by a hint of uncertainty.

'Two things which concern me slightly. First, knowing that this excursion involves considerable overland travel, don't we require both a guide and a translator to accompany us to the less hospitable regions? Second, do we know if the places we are venturing to are infested with bandits, cutthroats, wild beasts and disease?'

'We don't, but we will certainly find out. And when we arrive in South America we will hire the best guides, a cook and a couple of servants to travel with us.'

'I shall cook,' announced William.

Thia looked at him askance.

'I have done it before. And I have washed my own clothes before today. You forget, Thia, I am a poor writer and though I have a room in Mayfair, my means are very modest.'

Cynthia smiled. She always regarded William and her brother Algernon as equals and she had quite forgotten that fact.

'And where will we hire the horses?'

'I am sure local knowledge will be the best source of information.'

'I am beginning to favour the original suggestion of returning to England. Or perhaps we could sail to Bordeaux,' Algy said. 'They produce some wonderful cognac in that region. I'm sure Horatio would appreciate a few bottles.'

'Algy, I hope you are not serious, I cannot go alone. But with you, William – and Papa, of course – we will have an unforgettable vacation.'

'That is what I am afraid of!'

A sudden sharp bang echoed through the steamer. Every glass and piece of china, picture and ornament shuddered for a few seconds as if a rumbling volcano was about to explode. A moment later a plume of black smoke puffed from the dumb waiter which connected directly with the galley three decks below. Below decks a bell was ringing. Then the ship's general alarm sounded.

Within seconds, screams and cries could be heard issuing from all parts of the ship accompanied by the thumping of feet running along the decks. Within seconds, there was panic and all the steerage passengers were heading to the port side where the gangways were being set up.

'Nothing to be alarmed about, ladies and gentlemen,' the steward announced loudly, though his words were addressed to the smoke rather than the first-class passengers. 'The captain requests that everyone disembark the ship and assemble on the wharf. This is merely a precaution and once the problem is rectified you will be invited to return on board. Please hurry along. I'm sure this will not take long.

'Come along, ma'am. Please proceed to the gangway and remain on the wharf side for further instructions.'

'But I have not yet eaten breakfast,' Thia said.

'Breakfast will be served as soon as the problem is rectified.'

'And what is the problem,' Algernon asked.

'Don't know, sir, but Captain says it will be rectified.'

Algernon managed to control his smile as he turned to the steward. 'And if the same thing happens at sea, are we all to be ushered out into the lifeboats until the problem is rectified?'

'Captain's orders, sir. I'm only passing on the message.'

'Very well, but I trust this is not a taste of things to come!'

In the corner of the dining saloon, Mr Euan Davies was unmoved by the commotion. Sitting beside a port-side window, stroking his moustache, he watched the exodus of passengers belching from the side of the ship, pushing and shoving, clambering over each other down the gangways, to reach the safety of the wharf. Once on terra firma they milled around looking back at the ship, searching for their loved ones; women wailing and children crying at the sight of their parents' panic. In the meantime, the port authorities were at a loss as to how to contend with the sudden crowd of foreigners let loose on their dock.

'Bring me a fresh pot of tea, please, steward,' the man said, the lilt of his accent more evident.

'Certainly, Mr Davies.'

'Any idea how long this will take?' he asked softly.

'Not long I would think and it should not affect our sailing time.'

Fortunately, the fire in the galley was minor and quickly extinguished. Getting the passengers back on board however was a tedious matter as most had left in a hurry and had taken neither tickets nor identification with them. But despite the débâcle, the steamship sailed from Madeira at its scheduled time in the evening.

For most of the twenty-five first-class passengers, the day's events were the main topic of conversation over dinner. The mood was more than amiable as the champagne had been flowing freely for most of the day. Lord Beresford was happy to sample some of the local wine, Algernon was still pondering on whether they should have all headed for Bordeaux, while William was displaying the sketches he had made of the harbour.

From Madeira the PSNC's mail packet sailed to the Canary Islands and then south to the Islands of Cape Verde where it made only a brief stop to deliver its mail. That was the last stop before the long voyage crossing from the North to South Atlantic Oceans and visiting the ports of Rio de Janeiro and Monte Video. Here several of the first-class passengers left the ship, transferring to ferries to take them across the River Plate to the nearby town of Buenos Ayres situated on the opposite bank.

The weeks of the sea journey flew by quickly. Life was a daily pattern of meals, drinks, cigars, rubbers of whist, deck quoits, charades and impromptu entertainment. There was a string quartet and piano and William both sang and recited samples of his poetry, while other passengers presented various short performances. Despite the occasional cracked plate,

pieces of mismatched cutlery and the absence of the glam-
orous balls of such modern vessels as White Star's *Oceanic* or
Britannic, the ladies still appeared every night decked in their
diamonds and furs.

It was during the afternoons, when many passengers took
a nap, that Thia sat outside on a deck chair. Between reading
and watching the waves she sometimes wondered about the
stranger who had spoken to her when she was sick. The only
time she had seen him in the dining-room was in Madeira
when the fire broke out. Since then he had never graced the
dining saloon, not even for breakfast. Perhaps he ate
extremely early. She again wondered if he lacked the appropriate attire and asked her father to invite him to join them
privately. But each invitation sent to his cabin was returned
by the steward with a message of thanks saying Mr Davies
would be dining alone in his cabin that evening.

'I believe I won the wager, William,' Algernon said.

'And which one was that, pray tell?'

'Did you not wager that you would sketch the man's image
before we crossed the Equator?'

'By Jove, you are right. I did indeed. Now, for once, you are
one up on me. Perhaps I can make amends. I promise I will
speak with this reclusive Welshman and find out more about
him before we arrive at our destination.'

'Done,' said Algernon, shaking hands with his friend.

As the mail packet steamed east from Monte Video along the
turbid water of the Rio de la Plata, the lights of the town
dimmed then disappeared as it gathered speed.

'Do you know that the fresh water from this mighty river is
carried for more than three miles out to sea?'

William recognized the voice in the shadows, English but

with a hint of a Welsh accent. 'No, I did not.'

Standing in silence, the two men watched the line of wake left by the ship as it lengthened and the parallel tangents of smoke streaming from the funnels to disappear in the darkening sky. Even before the vessel had left the confines of the river's mouth, the shoreline had faded into obscurity.

'It is the first time I have ventured to this part of the ship,' William said. 'You must pardon me for encroaching on your privacy, sir, as I have noticed you prefer to spend time in your own company.'

'Solitude is a valuable thing,' the Welshman mused. 'I sometimes wonder about men in gaol. They never appreciate the solitude they have been granted.'

'Interesting. I must admit it is something I had never really considered. Yet as a writer, it is a condition I value greatly.'

'Ah, the writer,' he said. 'But aren't you also the artist? I have seen you sketching amongst the third-class passengers.'

'Then you are more observant than I and the rest of my party for we have not seen hide nor hair of you since Madeira.' William turned to look into the man's face. 'If you will forgive my boldness, I must take this opportunity to ask if you would care to sit for me. As an artist I would say you have an expressionful face.'

'Thank you, but I avoid mirrors, brass plates and brightwork and certainly do not wish to see a likeness of myself on paper.'

'Then I apologize for intruding on you in more ways than one.'

The night air was chilled by the wind blowing up from the Southern Ocean.

'Are you sailing to Valparaiso?'

'No, I will be disembarking at Punta Arenas or, as the

English call it – Sandy Point.'

'As we are also. Might I ask you the nature of your business there? My travelling companions were wondering. . . .'

'Sheep, sir. You may tell your companions, I am a sheep farmer.'

CHAPTER 6

Sandy Point – Strait of Magellan

The Pacific Steam Navigation's mail packet had been due to arrive at Punta Arenas at seven and Thia was out on deck expecting to catch her first glimpse of the port and the distant snow-capped peaks of the Andes.

But the troubled winds and currents, which have long been the nemesis of sailors entering the strait, behaved according to legend making the steamer's progress around Cape Virgenes slow. As the ship steamed into the eastern end of the Strait of Magellan and sailed across the broad body of water which separated the southern coast of the South American mainland from the island of Tierra del Fuego, the day dawned with a grey humour revealing a landscape which was far from handsome. To her right, from the ship's deck, were the featureless plains of the Patagonian pampas with neither a tree nor bush to break its steppe-like proportions. The sea was calm in the strait but like the sky, was also grey and unremarkable.

So this is Patagonia, Thia mused. Flat. Treeless. Monotonous – boring. She had read about it and should have been prepared, but somehow she was a little disappointed. At the same time, she was relieved that her companions were still breakfasting. During the three weeks of their journey, her excitement had mellowed from her days of planning the expedition.

Being the only person on the first-class section of the forward deck carried with it an air of loneliness. Was the isolation wafting from the land contagious? Wandering around to the port side, she wanted to get a good view of the island to the south. It was quite close now. Only a few miles separated Tierra del Fuego from the mainland, yet the terrain was quite different. Though hazy, the land rose steeply to ridges of high peaks, their tops lost in mist, and in contrast to the barren mainland, there appeared to be nowhere on the island not covered in trees. As the width of the strait narrowed, she observed columns of smoke rising straight from the valleys – grey struts supporting a canopy of cloud. But the dense, seemingly impenetrable forests ran right down to the water's edge with no beach or track to pass around it. How could anyone live in such an inhospitable place?

'So that is Tierra del Fuego!' she said out loud.

'Indeed it is.'

Thia started. She had thought she was alone.

The Welshman, leaning against the bulwarks, was gazing at the land of fire.

'It was first called Land of Smoke,' he said, 'but that later changed. It was argued that if there was smoke then there must also be fire.'

Thia glanced at him, but his eyes were fixed on the island.

'The local Indians revere fire and keep it burning continually.

'They even paddle their canoes through the maze of channels carrying a lighted fire in the bottom.'

She looked around to make sure he was addressing her. 'Have you visited the island before?'

'Several times,' he said, stepping forward to lean against the rail next to her.

She was surprised by his approach. 'What is over there?' she asked.

'Forests, swamps, a settlement or two, a prison, and now a gold mine.' He stared ahead, unblinking.

'What do you see?' she asked.

'Cold,' he answered. 'I see cold.'

She waited for him to explain but he did not continue. She wanted to hear more. Wanted to learn more about this man – at least where he was going and what his plans were. After spending weeks on board a ship together, this elusive stranger was still a mystery to her. If only he had conversed like this during the course of the voyage.

'I feel cold in this early morning breeze,' she said, 'but I do not see the cold. There is neither snow nor ice, nor any of the glaciers which I am told cut through the high valleys of the Cordillera.'

Again she waited, giving the man ample opportunity to respond but he offered no reply. By now the ship was steaming through the narrows. The nearest promontory was less than a mile distant.

'We will be leaving the ship at Sandy Point,' Thia said.

'Yes, I know.'

'And I heard you are also disembarking there.'

'Yes.'

Thinking it unlikely he would volunteer any further information, she continued, 'You have not asked why we have come to South America,' she said, hoping to rekindle the conversation.

'Why should I? No doubt you have your reasons.'

Thia's strained lips twisted in a smile balanced between elation and embarrassment. 'It was a whim that brought us here,' she said. 'A whim of mine – a desire to do something different and to explore a land few other people even know exists. From what I have read, Patagonia is one of the few regions on earth which can still boast that title.'

'It is indeed. It is also a place of contrasts. Stark. Cruel. Insensitive. Unforgiving. Beautiful. No doubt your friend, the artist, will appreciate those qualities.'

'Indeed he will. In fact we will all enjoy the diversity when we ride into the interior.'

The stranger turned sharply and faced her, his expression causing her to recoil.

'Take my advice, ma'am,' he said. 'Stay with the ship and sail north to Valparaiso.'

'We have not travelled almost halfway around the world to be deterred at this stage,' she said indignantly.

'Then if you must satisfy your whim, I advise you and your party to take great care. Patagonia is a dangerous place. It is a territory made up of the world's misfits and malcontents. Men who seek to make a fortune and men who have lost one. Men who have no respect for human life or property. Men on the run from the justice of their home countries and men who have no country to call their own. My advice to you, ma'am, is never trust a glib tongue and never underestimate the intelligence of a mute Indian. Never lend anything if you wish for it to be returned and never sleep at night without a knife or revolver under your blanket.' He paused. 'Can you shoot straight?'

'But of course,' Thia's quick reply smacked of pride. 'Huntingley is well stocked with pheasant and grouse, also deer and some wild goats. I go shooting at least once every week.'

'And I trust your companions are capable of defending you.'

'Mr Davies,' she said curtly, 'you are almost as negative as my elder brother in England. I get the distinct impression you are trying to be as off-putting as possible. From the picture you are presenting, I would expect to be robbed or murdered as soon as I step ashore.'

The Welshman shook his head.

Thia shivered, not from the cold air but from the unchanged expression on his face. She rubbed her hands and wished she had worn her gloves.

'And what makes you such an expert, Mr Davies?'

'I know the town. I was here in '77 when the riot took place. The convicts and soldiers mutinied, killing the captain of the garrison and all the officers. After fighting between themselves, they went on a rampage. Within two days they had razed Sandy Point to the ground, burnt every shop and house, leaving only a few of the stone buildings standing. They murdered and mutilated the prison guards. Raped the women. Shot children and babies and hung honest men from the beams in their own kitchens.'

'I did not know. And what happened to these villains?'

'When they had destroyed or looted everything of value they stole horses and rode out on to the pampas heading for Port Saint Julian on the east coast.

'There were one hundred and eighty mutineers. Most were ignorant fools following the orders of the ringleaders. They left Sandy Point loaded with the goods they had plundered, but with little water, no spare horses and no provisions. Most had never travelled inland before. They had no idea how harsh the pampas can be. They had plenty of guns which they had stolen, but took little ammunition, and most of them could not hunt their own food. Within days they started falling from exhaustion, or were fighting each other for survival. Needless to say before they covered the six hundred-mile journey only about forty survived, and when they were eventually tracked down near Port Desire they were barely alive.'

'Were they brought back to Sandy Point?'

Davies shook his head. 'There was no reason. The garrison had been burnt down. The prison guards murdered. They could not have survived the return journey and if they had stepped foot in the town the townsfolk would have torn them to pieces for the atrocities they committed. Instead, they were rounded up, taken to the port and shipped to Buenos Ayres.'

'What happened to them there?'

He sighed. 'They deserved to be hanged, but the authorities there could not agree on what to do with them so they were locked away and never brought to trial.'

'Were you living in Sandy Point at the time of the riot?'

'No, but I was not far away.'

'That was eight years ago. Has the town been rebuilt since then?'

'There are new dwellings. Rows of them like empty boxes. But there is little of substance there.'

'But what of the town's population?'

'Hundreds of defenceless people died or were killed in that riot and many of those who survived moved away. They had nothing left – no families, no possessions, no houses to live in. There was no reason to stay.'

'So who lives there now?'

'A melting pot of the lost souls which Punta Arenas has always attracted. The original settlers were seamen who were cast ashore from the old sailing ships and left to perish. Then there were the sealers and whalers who came and went. Now there are gold hunters. Also there are Indians, natives and gauchos, and Europeans on the run from justice in their own countries, even a few of the garrison mutineers who, when the riot ended, passed themselves off as law-abiding members of the community. You cannot be too careful who you trust in this place.'

How could she relate all this information to her brother and William before the steamer dropped anchor? she wondered.

'But you have returned?'

'Yes. I have business to attend to.'

'And may I ask where you are going once you leave the ship?'

Stroking his fingers through his broad moustache, he pointed south across the water to where the smoke columns were rising from the valleys. 'That is where I am going. Tierra del Fuego.'

As he spoke, the ship's engines shuddered and slowed.

'I believe we will be coming to Punta Arenas shortly. If you walk around to the starboard side you will see Sandy Point, as it was called. It is the gateway to this unfettered land which you have come so far to experience.' He inclined his head politely. 'If you will excuse me, I must prepare my baggage. I wish you and your companions – a pleasant vacation.'

Not knowing whether to thank him or berate him for dulling her spirits, Thia was about to respond, but before the chance arose Davies had turned into his cabin.

Rounding the deck to the other side of the ship, Thia was amazed at the change in the scenery which greeted her. The flat pampas had ended and wooded hill had taken its place. Ahead were beaches and a long strip of sandy land sticking out into the bay – the very point which Ferdinand Magellan had named Punta Arenas.

But the town which the English called Sandy Point was drab. More disappointing than the Welshman had described. A row of single-storey drab huts ran along the beach front. Running parallel behind them were more huts each with wooden walls and red corrugated iron roofs. Thia had thought that in eight years a reasonable town would have risen from the ashes of the razed settlement, but none existed. She swallowed hard.

For a few moments the sight of ships moored ahead of them encouraged her until the steamer drew a little closer. The plates on the hull of the iron ship were rusted and bent. All that remained was an empty shell half buried in the sand. Further along the beach the rotting remains of two wooden sailing ships poked up from the shallow water like the ribs of whale carcasses. The broken masts reflected the dying days of hemp and canvas fast fading from the high seas. What few timbers remained provided perches for thousands of black and white sea birds.

A shrill burst from the ship's whistle disturbed the cormorants which flapped and squawked but never relinquished their positions.

The ship shuddered as the anchor was let go and preparations were made to lower a boat.

Davies and his luggage had been in the first tender to leave the ship. The second was loaded with cargo and mail. By the time the Huntingley party was landed on the wooden wharf, the Welshman was heaving his baggage, rifles and saddle on to the back of a wagon. He never turned or looked back as he was driven up the main street into the town.

While waiting for the dogs and the rest of their luggage to

come ashore, Thia studied the faces of the local natives. Their skin was browner than a well-roasted joint but crumpled into masses of furrowed wrinkles. After her conversation on the deck that morning she was wary of anyone who approached and questioned the intentions of those who touched their fingers on the finely polished leather saddles. Her father seated himself on one of the travelling trunks and gazed around.

'Sheep, you say?' said Lord Beresford.

'That is what Mr Davies said.'

'Then that would explain many things. If he is a shepherd, he is probably not graced with the art of conversation.' He turned to William. 'I did not know Wales was renowned for its sheep.'

Thia was anxious to get going. 'Papa, you and William must wait here while Algy and I find a hotel or lodging-house – or a least a room – whatever the port of Sandy Point has to offer. Isaac can take charge of the luggage.'

Until then the young groom and Thia's maid had stood side by side gazing in disbelief at the town to which they had been delivered. How different it was from the docks in Liverpool.

Already the mountain of baggage bearing the Huntingley crest was attracting attention from the locals and though the town was alive with sleepy dogs, they were all leggy and smooth-haired, quite different to the shaggy Newfoundlands which were enjoying their new found freedom. Very soon a circle of natives clad in skin cloaks or woollen ponchos formed around them. Nervously, Ethel Thoroughgood did her best to assist, shooing away the inquisitive children. William, in his limited Catalonian Spanish attempted to conduct a conversation in which words of German, Portuguese and Araucanian confounded him.

Half an hour later, Thia returned with a triumphant look on

her face. She was accompanied by two wagons and with drivers. 'I have organized lodgings for the night, but as there is not a single inn or hotel in Sandy Point, I am afraid our accommodation is far from sumptuous. However, it is adequate and a meal will be prepared for us. We have the use of these wagons for the present and the shopkeeper will assist us in hiring some horses in the morning.'

'Excellent, Thia,' Lord Beresford said. 'I look forward to sleeping on a bed which is not moving.'

William's face was contorted with a pleased but sympathetic expression. 'Well, done, Thia. Trust you to come up trumps. Come along, Algy. Who knows what tomorrow will bring.'

'That is what I am worried about,' Algernon said.

It was nine o'clock before they finally sat down to dinner in a room at the back of a shop which was little bigger than the table at which the guests were sitting. Though comments about the shanty nature of the town, its inhabitants, the inadequacy of the sleeping accommodation and the lack of service, could not be avoided in the conversation, Algernon, in his own delightful way, endeavoured to make light of the situation, though Thia could sense he was in anguish inside. William, on the other hand, was completely at ease as always and was politely giving the appropriate support wherever necessary.

'In the morning the shopkeeper has offered to take us to a stable in town where we will be able to hire the necessary mounts for our expedition,' Thia announced.

'Excellent,' said Algy. 'Then we can begin our journey.'

They were interrupted by a visitor who appeared in the doorway.

'I am afraid if you hire those horses, the first night on the pampas, when you set them free to graze, they will gallop off and return to town. Unless you can identify each one individually, the proprietor will swear he has not seen them and make you pay again.'

'Mr Davies,' Thia said, rising to her feet. 'We did not expect to see you again. How did you find us?'

'That was not difficult in this town.'

'But I thought you were going to the island. Was there no boat today?'

'I learned that my need to visit Tierra del Fuego no longer existed. My business lies now to the north of here.'

'Splendid luck!' Lord Beresford cried. 'Then perhaps you would care to accompany us.'

The Welshman did not answer.

'We would be grateful for the benefit of your help and advice, sir,' Algernon said.

'Mr Davies,' Thia interrupted. 'We need to purchase supplies for our journey. We need horses for ourselves and our servants and mules for our luggage. Also we will need to engage one or more guides. Would you kindly advise us as to how many you think are necessary? And it would be preferable if you were to recommend them. Is that not so, Papa?'

'I leave this matter entirely in your hands, Thia.'

'And if you know of anywhere that can accommodate us in the interim, we would be most grateful for some guidance.'

All eyes were fixed on the Welshman's unemotional face. Thia watched as he studied the members of the Huntingley party each in turn – the doleful look on the face of Algernon, the nod of encouragement from William Ashley-Parker and the contented acceptance on the face of her father.

Thia's lips were spread in a large grin. She was delighted

that he had appeared so unexpectedly and thrilled with the prospect that he might be available to travel with them.

'Tomorrow I will take you to the estancia of a friend. It is only twenty miles from town. Señor Garcia runs many horses on his ranch; he will make you most welcome and you will be able to buy however many you require. I would suggest you will need twenty at least. On the way you can collect your provisions from the town. I see you have your own saddles but warn you that they may not suit the types of horses bred here. You may have seen them in the town.'

'I trust we will not be riding hacks?' Algernon said.

'No, sir. You will have some of the finest, fastest and most surefooted animals in the whole of South America. You will not be disappointed.'

'Then we must recompense you for your services,' Algernon said.

'I have invited you to the home of my friend and if you require, I will assist in the selection of horses, but I have not agreed to travel with you.'

'If it is a case of money. . . .'

Euan Davies's expression never changed nor did his voice alter in tone. 'I have already told you that my business now takes me north. I shall be heading out to the pampas. If you have no set route and are travelling in that direction I am prepared to ride along with you as your guide, so long as you follow the path I take. I assure you, as tourists you will see everything you want to see, but you will need to hire guides to act as cooks and help you hunt your food. At some point of the journey however, I will be leaving you.'

'Then state you price for half of the journey.'

'I want nothing from you. Be ready to leave here after breakfast tomorrow.' With no further words, the Welshman turned, the silver dagger stuck in the back of his belt glinting in the lamp light.

'A strange man,' Algernon said.

'A very interesting man,' William added.

CHAPTER 7

The Estancia

After being locked in a storeroom all night for fear they might be stolen or run away, the two Huntingley dogs were excited when they were released. Cavorting about like a pair of pups, they quickly attracted a mob of the long-legged mangy-looking locals who barked, sniffed and snapped at the newcomers. After half an hour exhausting themselves running up and down the street, the Newfoundlands returned to the wagons outside the shop where the travellers had lodged. Stacked with the saddles, rifles, tents and assorted cooking utensils which they had brought from England with them, William and Isaac were busy securing the loads with ropes, but every time they thought they had finished, Ethel would appear from the shop with additional blankets, trunks, saddle-bags or other items of hand luggage.

Thia watched. It seemed a considerable amount of luggage to transport but with an eight-week expedition ahead of them, all of it was essential.

A family of Indians squatting on the ground at the other

side of the street was also watching. Thia wondered what they were thinking and wished she could understand their guttural language. They looked friendly, though out of place on the street. The children naked; the adults barefoot, clutching their long fur *capas* around their shoulders. The soft fur was a little redder in parts than the colour of a fox. The rows of stitching indicated that several animal skins had been used to make each one. Thia remembered observing the Welshman when he arrived at the Liverpool docks. The cape he had worn around his shoulders had been similar.

Thia smiled at the women. They returned her smile, pointing and giggling at her riding habit and hat. Unlike the natives they had seen on the docks in England and in the foreign ports they had visited, these people were quite handsome with high cheekbones and aquiline noses, much more exaggerated than her own. The women's black hair was long and straight and tied back in two pigtails. Across their foreheads, they each wore a narrow brightly coloured woven fillet and around their necks, strings of blue beads.

The men's hair was not plaited and was longer than that of the women. Their faces, apart from daubs of red paint, were devoid of hair and even the women had removed their eyebrows which struck Thia as looking a little strange.

At the sound of another wagon rumbling along the street, the Newfoundlands barked excitedly. Thia waved to her father who was sitting next to the driver. Algernon, having cast off his jacket, was happily perched atop the sacks of rice, sugar, flour, onions and tinned foodstuffs which they had just purchased. On his face was the grin of a seven year old having just mastered the art of riding a bicycle. Amused by his friend's expression, William stopped what he was doing and applauded.

Thoroughgood, Thia's maid, smiled nervously. She had become quietly reserved since they had landed at the port. The order of things had become quite topsy-turvy and with no set rules or routine to follow, she found it all rather disturbing. The prospect of spending two months in the saddle was something she did not speak of.

Euan Davies, riding alongside the wagon, was sitting a fine horse – a bay mare. Not far behind him were three other horsemen – the guides Davies had hired for them. Besides knowing the pampas, its dangers and the best routes to take, these men would be responsible for setting up camp, cooking and hunting sufficient meat to feed everyone. Without successful hunters, the party would soon starve.

Circling around the riders was a new group of dogs – six smooth-coated, skinny canines, built like greyhounds, three greys, two whites and one spotted.

Looking down the street towards the sea, Thia saw another rider – an Indian woman. As she neared the wagons, she, too, reined in her mount and stopped but did not dismount. Sitting astride her horse, her big toes rested on the simple stirrups. She wore a plain calico mantle which was fastened at the waist with a beaded belt and the typical fur *capa* around her shoulders, secured at the neck with a large silver clasp. Even in the saddle, she looked very tall. She neither spoke nor smiled nor watched anyone in particular, but it was obvious to Thia that this Indian was now also one of their party. Was she a cook or the wife of one of their guides? Thia wondered. No doubt she would find out shortly.

As the dust on the street settled, she could see all the way to the calm waters of the Magellan Strait. Apart from the old wrecks, washed by the strong tides, the anchorage at Sandy Point was empty. The Pacific Steam Navigation Company's steamship had sailed. It would be two weeks before it returned from Valparaiso. Thia and her party's commitment to Patagonia was sealed and if all went well they would not be back for several weeks. Only then would they rejoin the steamer for their return voyage to England.

Meeting the Welshman had proved fortuitous. If he could find some suitable accommodation for them and procure a quantity of good horses as efficiently as he had hired the local guides, then everything augured well for the adventure on which they were about to embark.

The estancia which Davies took them to was situated ten miles from the town. The stone-built white farmhouse was considerably older than most of the buildings in the town itself. It had been constructed in the Spanish style and was set in formal gardens with roses, lawns, trimmed hedges, and palm trees. Mature poplars lined the driveway and acted as a wind break from the westerly wind. It was single-storey and built around a courtyard with arches and a covered walkway leading to a schoolhouse and gaucho quarters. It was a fine home and could easily have graced any city in southern Europe.

Their host, Señor Garcia, greeted Davies with a warm embrace. He was a quietly spoken gentleman with a smooth complexion, despite his years, and bright inquisitive eyes, a man obviously revered by all those who worked for him. Over a shirt with billowing sleeves, he wore a hand-woven waistcoat and around his waist a broad leather belt embedded with many pieces of silver, the size and shape of a silver dollar. A large curved, silver-handled dagger was stuck down the back of his belt, and like the Welshman, he had a thick moustache which drooped down from the corners of his mouth, reaching almost to his chin. His wavy hair, once black was now variegated in shades of grey.

In good broken English, he explained that like many other inhabitants of Patagonia, he had come from the Canary Islands as a child but had lived in the region for most of his life. His parents had established the estancia and he had continued in the family tradition – breeding beef cattle. His main love however was for the Criollo – the wild horses of the pampas. His eyes sparkled as he spoke about them.

'They are the descendants of the Spanish war horses which were brought to the New World in the 1500s. Centuries ago a handful were released on to the pampas. Now there are thousands. They survived because of their strength, hardiness and longevity. They are courageous and love their freedom. And like the horsemen of the pampas, they fear nothing.

'Tomorrow you will see some of them. The gauchos, will round them up and bring them into a corral for you to choose,' he said. 'But tonight you relax, drink wine, and eat beef cooked on the *asado* over an open fire. You will enjoy. I guarantee.' Señor Garcia was gracious, kindly and unassuming and Lord Beresford found his company most charming.

The grand farmhouse was large with lots of airy room, all furnished with the most elegant highly polished furnishings from Europe. Silver and porcelain ornaments graced the shelves and dressers. There were several oil lamps in every room with carved marble, coloured glass or silver bases. Pictures of horses adorned the walls, together with framed embroideries and preserved flowers which his wife had created over the years. The bookcases in his compact library overflowed with literature in Spanish, German, Dutch and English, with volumes in several other languages. Everywhere Thia looked there were items of interest.

Leaving the men to their drinks, Thia soaked for half and

hour in a warm bath then, relaxing on to the feather mattress of the old four poster bed, would have fallen asleep had it not been for the call of the cuckoo clock on the wall.

That evening the whole party sat down at one long table. It was lighted by two elegant candelabras and was set with silver cutlery and crystal glasses. But despite the elegant setting, the meal was served by the hosts' granddaughters and proved to be a homely affair. Everyone agreed that the beef was the most succulent they had ever eaten. When the meal was over, the *yerba maté* was passed around the table. Sucked from a gourd through a silver straw, they learned it was not only a social custom, but a refreshing and invigorating drink, rather like tea.

Señor Garcia was delighted to relate some of his many experiences and was anxious for his guests to stay longer so he could show them the thousands of head of stock he ran over the huge unfenced property. Lord Beresford was particularly interested but apologized that on this occasion they could not delay their expedition. After more drinks and cigars, the group bade each other goodnight.

This was to be their last night sleeping in a bed for a long time.

The following morning was fine and fresh and from the glass windows in the dining-room Thia noticed clouds of dust rising as the Criollo horses were driven in to the corral. After eating breakfast, it was time to select the animals they would need for their expedition.

Including the two servants, there were six in the group from Huntingley, plus the three gauchos who had been hired as their guides, also the Welshman and the Indian woman. Eleven riders in all. For a journey of several hundred miles and spanning six to eight weeks, they would need at least forty horses for their own requirements. As there were no pack-mules available for carrying the tents and provisions, Davies suggested the number should be increased to forty five. It seemed an exceedingly large mob, but with the amount of baggage and quantity of provisions they were taking, there would be few spare mounts. No one argued about the number.

A cloud of dust hovered over the corral as the horses moved around it. The majority were dun coloured, dingy-brown or sandy grey, but there were a few blacks and chest-nuts scattered amongst them. The Criollo horses' legs were short, their hocks low-set and their black hoofs, appeared sound. They were of medium length with rather short heads, but they had muscular necks, strong shoulders, and broad chests. Thia and her companions were immediately impressed. They were not the most handsome animals they had seen, but they certainly looked powerful and built for endurance. The gauchos working with them were also remarkable in their horsemanship.

Confined in the corral the horses were skittish and uneasy, snorting and throwing their heads and flashing their teeth. When one of the gauchos walked amongst them they were wary.

Observing from the fence, the group eagerly cast their eyes around the mob discussing their obvious qualities. Neither Señor Garcia nor the Welshman said anything during the selection process though they eyed each animal carefully.

Choosing their mounts took longer than that of the pack animals. Thia picked a spirited mare, one which immediately caught her eye. Once selected the horseman spun the *lazo* and dropped it on over the horse's neck. Immediately it felt the rope touch it, it came to a stop and stood quietly.

Algy and William sought advice from Señor Garcia. He reminded them politely that is was unlikely they would use the same mount every day, so choosing a specific horse was not necessary. He assured them all his horses were intelligent, durable and hardworking. How the horse performed was up to the rider.

'They will not trust the rider until the rider proves himself trustworthy,' he said. It was going to be a challenge.

Several individual horses were singled out by the Englishmen and the young Huntingley groom was delighted when he was allowed to pick his own mount. Davies gave advice whenever asked but, as usual, was economical with his words.

The most difficult proposition was to select a quiet mount which would accept a side-saddle for Ethel Thoroughgood. Eventually, a small horse which had been hand-reared by Señora Garcia was brought from his stable. Though it had never carried its rider aside before, it did not object to the feel of the unusual saddle or distribution of the rider's weight. It was in good condition, as it was ridden regularly by one of Señor Garcia's granddaughters. As Ethel would not be hunting or running down prey, it was thought it would be capable of carrying her on the days they were travelling.

It took three hours to distribute and load all the baggage and equipment into canvas sacks and secure them to the backs of the ten pack horses. Even then, two of the animals did not take kindly to their load, rearing and kicking until the girth were loosened. Replacements were soon made.

Around noon, after handshakes and embraces, the party set off. Thia, her father and twin brother plus William Ashley-

Parker, made up the main group. Mindful of Ethel
Thoroughgood's limitations, Isaac, the young groom
followed behind, while the three gauchos and Euan Davies
drove the mob of pack animals and spare horses. The Indian
woman trailed at the rear with eight dogs trotting along
beside her. The pair of Huntingley dogs revelled in their new
found canine company, but the lanky ostrich dogs, like their
owners, appeared churlish and uncommunicative. After a
while, the smooth-haired dogs ran ahead leaving the long-
haired Newfoundlands padding alongside Thia and her
father.

After spending only one night at the home of Señor Garcia,
heading back through the centre of the strait's town reminded
them all how depressing Sandy Point was. The streets were
dusty and dilapidated and every shop appeared to be a bar
where men drank from morning till night.

Eight years before the town had been home to 800 people
but with the riot, that number had fallen considerably. Only
recently was it beginning to grow again. But, almost all the
new houses were built with timber walls and had red iron
roofs and only when they rode through the main plaza did
they see any new stone buildings under construction.

Clattering across the paved square, the riders were met by
strange looks. It was not unusual for a group of gauchos to
pass through heading out to the pampas or the Gallegos
River. Or for a family of *capa*-clad Indians to ride into town
leading pack-horses loaded with bundles of ostrich feathers
to trade at the local store. But this group of English aristocrats
dressed in their smart riding gear were out of place in this
forgotten outpost at the bottom of the world.

Thia was eager to speak with the Welshman and learn more
about him. That opportunity had not been available at the

estancia as he had not joined them for dinner. Offering no reason for leaving and not tendering his apology, he had returned to Sandy Point soon after they arrived. When he eventually returned it had been very late and he had made no account of himself. Thia was not used to such behaviour and his non-communication irked her.

During the evening she had asked Señor Garcia if he knew why the Welshman had left. The rancher did not know, nor did the man's absence bother or surprise him. He admitted that he had heard that a few days ago an Indian had been killed at Peckett's Harbour and his horses stolen. He doubted that this event had any bearing on Davies going to town. He said this sort of thing was not unusual on the pampas – a place inhabited by a population of wild and undisciplined characters.

CHAPTER 8

The Gauchos

Leaving Sandy Point behind them the party headed into a thinly wooded area cut by several waterways. Being mid-summer, the streams were narrow with only a trickle of water running down the centre of them, but the broad expanse of soil and vegetation which had been brutally excavated and carried to the sea was evidence of the powerful force which flooded the watercourses each spring fed by the melt-waters of the mountains.

From the woods they dropped on to an open plain dotted with patches of trees. Then the land rose again into dense forest and they were forced along a narrow stony strip running along the Magellan Strait. With the tree-line running to the water's edge, they were forced into single file. They followed the track for three hours at times splashing through the shallow salty water. When the hills ended and the forest thinned out, they were all relieved.

Ahead of them was open prairie and in the distance another ridge of hills. As they spurred their horses Thia watched the three men whom Davies had hired as their guides. They were gauchos – horsemen of the pampas – who, without a horse were likened to men without legs. They spoke little, either to each other or anyone else, their comfortable silence reflecting the solitude of the Patagonian plains. Though unassuming and reserved, they were all alert and intelligent and skilful hunters with either the *lazo* or *bolas*.

Jose was the most striking of the three. He was a handsome man of about forty, a Spaniard, who had come to South America as a young adventurer. He had spent the last twenty years on the pampas. His hair was blue black, short and wavy and he wore a soft felt hat when he was riding. His clothing was clean but unusual, a military shirt and broad Turkish style trousers. Thia later learned he had deserted from the Spanish Army. When he walked he moved gracefully and when he smiled, his eyes flashed. He appeared shy and said little, though his command of English was reasonably good.

Carlos was quite different. He was a big man – the height and build of a Tehuelche Indian and just as muscular and strong. He could pick up a male guanaco and throw it on to the saddle single-handed. William nicknamed him *The Titan*. Like the Patagonian Indians, he had dark eyes which smiled when he smiled. He laughed a lot. He wore a fur *capa* and the traditional *chiripa*, a type of loose kilt wrapped between his loins and fastened at the waist. His cheeks and arms bore deep scars. Thia later learned that he had wrestled a wild puma and killed the beast with his bare hands. His mother was a native Indian, his father a Portuguese sailor, but that was all he knew of them. Carlos's eyesight was remarkable.

Martin, the third guide, was from Peru. He was a short, stocky fellow, the shortest of the three guides. To compensate, his boots had several extra layers of leather nailed to the soul and heel. He was easy to remember as he always wore a gaily coloured poncho and a black bowler hat. His eyes were close set and he appeared sullen and he spoke even less than the others. But when asked to do anything he was always willing to work. Davies said that Martin could skin a guanaco in a matter of minutes; quicker than any other man he had seen. He had ridden the length of South America and crossed the Cordillera from the Pacific coast of Chile several times. He had been in Patagonia for five years. He spoke mainly in Spanish.

Each man had two ostrich dogs running with him.

'Our three guides are colourful characters,' Algy said innocently.

Wlliam laughed. 'You are learning, my friend.'

Thia was riding between the two men. 'I don't know what to make of the Indian woman.'

'She has a beautiful face and her bone structure is superb,' William said.

'I think she looks rather aloof,' Algy said.

'I think you must look more closely. I sense an immense sadness beneath her polished mahogany skin.'

'Then you must capture that on paper,' Algernon said.

'I would love to draw her, but I fear I may offend her. She probably speaks no English and like many aboriginals, might be afraid that if I copy her likeness on paper it would take something from her soul.'

'Then perhaps you can sketch her when she is not aware,' Thia said.

'But that would be dishonest.'

'Yes, you are right,' Thia said. 'I wonder what her purpose is on this trip and who she is with. If she is not the wife of one of the guides, then who is she?'

102

Much of the time Davies chose to ride at the back of the group while Jose, Carlos and Martin often galloped off ahead, at times veering left or right, always alert. The Indian woman usually trailed at the back not communicating with anyone.

Across the plain there were scattered pockets of beech trees and the ground carried a haze of grass though it had already turned brown. As they had not yet reached the true pampas, there were no herds of guanacos to hunt, but a male rhea which had been sitting on a nest was disturbed by the dogs. Though not as big as its African cousin, the Patagonian ostrich was brown and agile. It ran with his neck outstretched and its flightless wings spread. The dogs gave chase but it out-ran them and escaped into the trees. After calling them back, Jose retraced his tracks and located the nest. It contained fifteen eggs, each one the equivalent of eight hen's eggs.

A few miles ahead rose a steep ridge with no obvious way to get around it. The riders had no alternative but to go over the top. It was covered with thick forest which in most parts was too dense to penetrate but the guides knew a path used by the Indians. It was an extremely steep climb made more difficult by fallen trees and loose rocks underfoot. The horses were used to such terrain, but Ethel was almost unseated every time her horse stumbled.

At the very top of the ridge there was a clearing and they could see for miles. From here they got their first glimpse of the pampas, the seemingly flat plain stretching north as far as the eye could see. To the west were the irregular snow-covered crags of the Cordillera – the tail end of the Andes mountain chain which stretched like a backbone down the full length of South America.

Breaking for a drink and a biscuit, Thia gazed back in the direction from which they had come. The sun was glistening across the Strait of Magellan and on the southern bank the tree-covered mountains rose into Tierra del Fuego's private cover of cloud.

From the top of the ridge the port of Punta Arenas looked idyllic basking along its broad stretch of sandy beach with several ships gracing its quiet waters. Then she remembered the state of the rusted wreck and the derelict wooden hulls of the sailing ships resting in the sand. The ship which had arrived in port that day was the Chilean coastguard vessel. It patrolled those waters in case of uprisings. Sandy Point was hardly a popular tourist destination.

Descending the ridge on the northern side was almost harder than climbing up. With the steep decline and the loose stones slipping from beneath the horses' hoofs each rider had to lay back across his mount's rump and pray that the horse was sure footed. Though she made a gallant effort, it was impossible for Ethel to remain seated so it was necessary for her to scramble down on foot with Isaac's help.

'This will never do,' Thia mumbled to herself, as the others waited for almost half an hour for the pair to reach the bottom.

For several hours they rode on, their progress dictated by the pace of the slowest member of their party.

Davies said nothing, but Thia sensed his frustration. By mid-afternoon he suggested they stop for the night. For the three gauchos, setting up camp was a familiar job, but for the aristocrats unfamiliar with the new duties, it was a routine they would have to master. Confronted with so many canvas packs, it was a daunting proposition.

As each horse was relieved of its load, the Welshman said they were to release them.

'But surely they will get lost,' Thia said.

'They will not go far. There is plenty of feed for them here. Because the horses cannot eat while we are travelling, we set them loose at night to find their own grazing. Often they wander five or ten miles from the campsite, but they always stay together in a knot. When we find them, the *madrinas* – the bell-mares – lead them back. The only danger is from the packs of wild horses. The stallions will fight to steal mares and if they succeed it is impossible to get them back. But the wild horses roam in the foothills of the Cordillera to the west, so here we are safe.'

'And where are we heading from here?'

'To the north-west. Tomorrow night we will camp beside a lake. From there you will see the mountains more clearly. Lake Otway will provide the opportunity to bag some game before we move up to the higher ground. It is a slow climb. The pampas is like a great staircase, the flat plateaux, which seem to stretch forever, are formed in steps which rise from the coast to the Cordillera.'

'How long will it take us?'

'I cannot say.' He paused for a moment before he spoke. 'Your party is a big one – too big, I fear, and you will need a considerable quantity of meat to feed everyone. The days you spend hunting, you do not proceed on your journey. Jose and Carlos are good hunters. They will help you. Martin is an excellent guide who knows the mountains well. Those three men will take you wherever you want to go.'

'But I thought you would travel with us.'

'I did not promise to stay with you. My business is pressing and you are too slow.'

Thia prickled. She was acutely aware of that fact and had joked with her brother and William that they resembled a travelling circus packing up their tents and belongings and moving everything everyday. Algernon had agreed, playfully reminding her that this had been her idea of adventure. She was concerned for her father who would not sleep well on the hard ground. He would never complain but it was obvious to her that he was not relishing the prospect and had already passed several comments about the comfortable accommodation which Señor Garcia had provided for them. He had enjoyed sampling the local wine and beef and regretted that there had been no time to ride out and inspect the cattle. He had particularly enjoyed sitting in the evening listening to Garcia's granddaughters reading to him in English. Thia realized he regretted having no grandchildren of his own.

Then she thought of her maid, Ethel Thoroughgood – a true and faithful servant who had served the family for over twenty years. But Goody was completely out of place in Patagonia and was the main culprit for their delays. Though loath to admit it, Thia knew that Horatio had been right; the pampas is no place for a lady's maid. She was angry because he was right and she was guilty of forcing her maid to come along against her will. Ethel not only slowed the party down but she also took up much of Isaac's time which could be put to better use.

But what could be done? She could not send the woman back to Sandy Point alone to await the next steamer and she had no intention of making the return journey with her.

Carlos prepared the meal – a nine-month-old lamb cut in two halves and stretched over an iron frame angled across the fire.

The sheep was a parting gift from Señor Garcia and when roasted was as succulent as any lamb eaten at Huntingley. It was their first meal under the stars but the last domesticated meat they would eat for the next eight weeks.

The ostrich eggs were a special treat. They all watched as Martin carefully drilled a hole in the top of one and removed part of its content. A little sugar and a splash of brandy were stirred into it before it was placed upright into the embers of the fire. When cooked it tasted like Christmas custard. After the meal, the *maté* was passed around, everyone drinking from the same gourd as was the South American custom. The tea was surprisingly refreshing.

A chill wind from the south blew through the camp replacing the warmth of the summer's day. It channelled down on them from the ridge but the pockets of beeches provided ample wood and a large fire warmed them. Being sore and tired, Lord Beresford, Algernon and William went to their beds fairly early. From now on their feather pillows were replaced by saddles, bedsteads by horse rugs, and sheets and blankets by furs.

Neither the three gauchos nor Davies seemed tired. Thia felt wide awake so, with her two Newfoundlands for company, she relaxed beside the camp-fire.

'What use are they?' Davies asked abruptly, looking at her dogs whose ears occasionally pricked to the crackle of the burning wood.

'They are Newfoundlands,' she said.

'I did not enquire as to their breed, ma'am, but to their ability.'

Thia stood corrected. 'They are excellent swimmers,' she said, gently lifting Byron's foot and displaying the duck-like webbing running between his toes. 'Besides, they have a good nose – equal to most hounds, and they are intelligent and make fine companions. We have had Newfoundlands at Huntingley for several generations.'

Davies's expression did not change.

'You do not like them?' she enquired.

'It is not a question of liking them, ma'am, it is a question that they are large and will have big appetites. Those two dogs will consume as much meat as one person in your party.'

Thia could not disagree. 'But our three guides have two dogs each and they are large and very energetic and will also require feeding.'

'But those dogs will earn their keep. Carlos's dog can out-run a rhea. And the others will run down a herd of guanaco – the long-necked llama. You will see big herds of those animals as we travel. And in the coming weeks, apart from some birds and waterfowl from the lakes, ostrich and guanaco meat will be your main diet. Without the hunting dogs, you will all go hungry.'

'I am sure my dogs will prove their worth,' she said. 'And if nothing else they will keep me warm at night.' She reached out her hand and ran her fingers through her dog's thick black coat. Byron responded, nuzzling his cold nose into her hand. Smiling, in response to the dog's affection, Thia turned to continue the conversation, but the Welshman had risen and slipped back into the darkness.

She could hear her maid, Goody, talking with the young groom, and feared that the first day's ride had taken its toll on her. Isaac, on the other hand, was eager and proving competent in any job he was given.

With a guanaco skin draped around her shoulders, the young Indian woman sat cross-legged, alone in the darkness. Swaying slightly, she hummed softly and did not change her pose even when the Welshman leaned down and placed a piece of meat in her hand. Squatting down at her side, they sat watching the sparks dancing from the fire each time Carlos threw another log on it. As the smoke swirled skyward, the sparks competed with the myriad of stars which dotted the black sky.

One by one the gauchos abandoned the fire and lay down under their furs. Lying awake, Thia listened to her brother and William. They spoke for a while then all was silent. She watched the fire from her open tent till it slowly died, the embers burning to a white ash. And when her eyes were beginning to close, she noticed the Welshman reach his hand into his shirt and retrieve a piece of cloth. Unfolding it on his lap, he took out a long black quill feather. He stared at it for a while then stroked it gently across his cheek.

Sitting a few yards away, the Indian woman was also watching him. The moonlight reflected in her tears revealed her closely guarded emotion.

CHAPTER 9

Lake Otway

Though everyone was up at dawn, it was three hours later before the party rode out. Lolloping along beside the riders, the two big dogs kept an easy pace, their long black hair swaying with every stride.

After an hour in the saddle, Thia spurred her horse and joined the Welshman who had ridden ahead.

'You ride like a man,' he said.

'Yes,' she said with an air of pride.

Ahead, the terrain had changed again. The pockets of beech trees had disappeared replaced by low scrub and grass. The ground undulated gently but the further they rode the more sparse the vegetation became and the small hillocks slowly flattened out. To the east were a series of freshwater lakes surrounded by swamps, but being summer many had dried out and were hard enough to ride over. But they had turned from the lowland and were heading north and west across the broad plains. Now there was barely a bush and not a single tree in sight. To their left were the hazy purple peaks of the

110

Andes, their rugged contours softened by the perpetual snow of the icefields.

'How far is it to the mountains?' Thia asked.

'Several days' ride. The distance is deceptive.'

'And when your business is finished will you return to Sandy Point and sail back to England.'

'I think not.'

As they unpacked the cooking utensils from one of the canvas packs, Ethel Thoroughgood chose her words carefully. 'I know it's not my place to say, ma'am, but there's something mighty strange about that Mr Davies. He only speaks when he's spoken to – a bit like a child. Never passes the time of day. Seems preoccupied with something, if you ask me. Like he's carrying the weight of the world on his shoulders.'

'I think you have summed him up in a nutshell, Goody. I had come to the same conclusion myself.'

'And if you'll pardon me for saying, ma'am, I think that Indian lass's behaviour is downright odd too. I've never known anyone keep themself to themself as much as she does. Not natural in my mind.'

'But we are not in Nottinghamshire now, Goody.'

'No, ma'am, I'm afraid we are not,' she said emphatically. 'Now Mr William – he's a real gentleman, even though he writes them plays for the theatre. He don't mind passing the time of day with the likes of me and young Isaac. In fact I heard the pair of them talking and saying they thought Mr Davies was following some tracks, and how they'd noticed he was always on the lookout. Cautious like.'

'Listening to other people's gossip leads to no good,' Thia said sternly.

'Yes, ma'am. Sorry, ma'am.'

'However, there is no need for you to concern yourself. Mr Davies tells me we are indeed following tracks. The Indians visit Sandy Point one or twice a year to trade their feathers and furs for tobacco and supplies. As for Mr Davies keeping a sharp look out – I think all of our guides are being vigilant. They are looking for game. After all we do have to eat.'

When Ethel excused herself, Thia wondered if perhaps she had not been observing the Welshman closely enough. Was he really following old Indian tracks? And was it just ostriches and guanaco he was constantly scanning the prairie for?

Across the expanse of Lake Otway the snow-covered peaks on the horizon glowed pink in the early morning light. The air was still and clear, the sky crisp blue from end to end. It would have been idyllic but for the squawking of tens of thousands of penguins which had come ashore the previous evening and the thousands of chicks now being left in the sandy hollows and ditches some yards from the beach. The young birds still covered in down had been hatched in spring at the time when a flush of minute flowers bloomed amongst the sparse vegetation. Now the fluffy chicks looked bigger than their parents and were twice as hungry.

As the dogs ran to the lake to swim, hundreds of waddling penguins scattered, clamouring over each other in their wild dash for the safety of the water. Once in the lake they frolicked and dived, splashing and squeaking – the noise of the rookery being no less reduced.

With their broad webbed feet and waterproof coats, the two Newfoundland dogs swam almost as fast as the flightless birds.

The constant chirping and chatter continued late into the evening and resumed at dawn when the adults appeared from their burrows and waddled down to the lake to go fishing.

'I have never been woken by such a cacophony of cries. It's either a dozen donkeys braying or the gates of Bedlam have been thrown open. How is one expected to sleep in such a location?'

'Good morning, Algy,' Thia said. 'Perhaps I should complain about your snoring, Brother dear, that is far more of a distraction in the early hours of the morning.'

Algernon Beresford grunted as he stirred his porridge. 'And what, may I ask, is on the agenda for today?'

'A day's shooting. We must supply ourselves with sufficient meat to last for the next three days. Mr Davies tells me that we will find a plentiful supply of wildfowl anywhere around the lake but they are more plentiful at the other side. Mr Davies assures me the duck are as tasty, if not more succulent, than those in the English marshes. We should easily be able to bag a dozen brace between us. It will be a good day's sport.'

'I shall enjoy a little shooting,' Lord Beresford said, 'but I shall not ride far from here.'

'Then Martin will accompany you and you must take Isaac and Byron.'

Byron was an excellent dog to take on a shooting party. Like all Newfoundlands, he was an excellent retriever as well as strong swimmer. It wouldn't matter where a bird fell, the dog would locate it and return it safely. Bella, on the other hand, would quickly recover the downed fowl but had a habit of depositing it on the shore then proceeding to lick its wounds, pawing as if in an attempt to revive it. She only returned when she was called.

It was a perfect day for a ride and Thia was looking

forward to a fine excursion. As to the sporting aspects of the day's shoot, in an area teeming with so much birdlife, it was likely a blind man could fire small shot and bring down a brace or two.

While Thia and the others headed off for the lake's eastern shore. Lord Beresford accompanied by Isaac and Martin rode west. From the penguin rookery it was only five or six miles to a pocket of marshland which was home to dozens of varieties of birds and fowl. It was only a short ride which Lord Beresford was looking forward to.

They were a motley group. The English peer in his smartly tailored riding outfit; the groom in breeches, a cord shirt and woollen waistcoat; and Martin, the Peruvian, in his brightly coloured poncho and his bowler hat pushed hard down on his head, his long black hair trailing out behind him as he rode. With the tips of his shaggy black hair glowing bronze in the morning light, Byron, Lord Beresford's Newfoundland trotted along beside the horses while the gaucho's two ostrich dogs streaked off ahead.

Not far from the camp they skirted some marshy ground and Martin was careful to guide them around the flat areas of soft green. In places, large tracts of moss veiled spongy layers of black peat whose insidious dangers were not obvious. Riding along the slightly higher ground about half a mile from the water's edge, they quickened their pace, cantering along quite comfortably in silence.

Lord Beresford set the pace. He could see for miles but there were no trees, only low shrubs on the lake's edge. Across the broad stretch of water the complete horizon was spanned by the snow-capped Cordillera, the inverted image of the mountains mirrored perfectly on the shining surface.

With the wind blowing directly across the lake from the icy waters of the western strait, the air was crisp and cold. There was little grass as there was no topsoil to support it. The only animal they saw was a Patagonian hare. It sat on its haunches and regarded the riders before flicking its ears and hopping away. But above their heads the air was filled with birds of all descriptions, waterfowl, ibises, ducks and cranes all flying to and from their feeding grounds.

Suddenly Martin cried out. *'Tucu-tucu! Cuidado!'* His tone was urgent and abrasive. Lord Beresford, however, had just spurred his horse to a gallop. He was enjoying the ride, the fresh air in his lungs and the freedom of the pampas. Either he did not hear or he did not understand the call and did not stop.

Directly ahead was a flat patch of ground which the pampas rats had claimed as their home. It was pitted with numerous deep holes which led down to a network of subterranean passages. But unlike English rabbits who usually dug into the sides of a hillock, these rodents burrowed straight down into the hard ground.

When its hoof lodged in one of the burrows, the animal stumbled and horse and rider went down heavily. Lord Beresford took the full weight of his mount on his right leg as it fell.

Martin pulled up in an instant and was quickly on the ground beside him. Isaac had also not understood the warning but had correctly interpreted the tone and taken heed of it. He quickly dismounted and went to attend to the horse.

The English lord's pain was excruciating as the gaucho gently straightened his leg.

'Damn stupid thing to do,' Lord Beresford said, trying to make light of the matter. 'Give me your arm, young man and help me to my feet.'

But Martin would not let him rise and pressed him back to the ground. Rolling up the fur from his saddle, he placed it beneath the aristocrat's head and despite the pain and protestations, examined the injured limb.

'Fine pickle this is!'

'Leg not broken,' Martin announced, with a broad smile on his round face. 'This ankle bad. Knee bad too. Take leg to doctor. No ride. I go to camp. Make litter. Carry man back. You stay here,' he said to Isaac. 'Watch for sun and vultures. Drink water. I come back soon.'

Though he was not tall in stature and not a young man, the gaucho leapt on to his horse with the agility of a youth of eighteen and within minutes nothing could be seen of him but a cloud of dust disappearing along the shores of the lake.

Ethel Thoroughgood was the only person who had remained in the camp after the others had gone shooting and, not expecting to see any of them back until late in the afternoon, she was shocked to see Martin galloping back. Unable to fully explain what had happened, Martin quickly disassembled one of the tents and fastened the poles and canvas on to the back of one of the spare horses. Then he bundled up a pile of skins, straps, ropes and harnessing and loaded them on to another. In less than ten minutes he had everything that was necessary to make a litter to transport the man on.

Leading two pack horses meant his return journey was tediously slow and it was more than an hour before he got back to the injured man. With Isaac's help, it took another half an hour to construct a litter and harness it securely to the back of one of the pack horses.

By this time Lord Beresford's right leg had swollen

painfully. Dexterously the Indian cut through the riding breeches and sliced down the polished leather of his riding boot to remove it. By now, the knee, swollen with fluid, was immovable.

Lord Beresford was a big man both in height and weight and lifting him on to the litter was not easy. As he lay in a semi-reclined position, he considered the journey back to the camp. Being dragged by the horse, the ends of the poles would bump over every stone and piece of uneven ground. And with only the fur skins folded beneath his leg to provide any cushioning, he was not looking forward to the five-mile journey. But he had no choice and never complained about the pain though he had already drained the silver flask of brandy which he carried in his breast pocket. It helped a little.

After three days by the lake, the party were all sick of the sound of the penguins and utterly fed up with the diet of wildfowl. A decision had to be made. It would be impossible for Lord Beresford to ride any further and the whole expedition was in danger of being abandoned.

Euan Davies had already left. The Indian woman also. The Welshman had waited for two full days, even though he had been anxious to move on. He said his business was pressing and he could wait no longer. He offered to take any of the party if they wanted to accompany him but no one accepted. They wanted to remain together. Thia was angry, frustrated and disappointed. She had begged him not to leave but he had made up his mind.

Till now the family had agreed to stay together but it was obvious that Lord Beresford needed to see a doctor and William offered to ride back to Sandy Point and return with one. But Algernon felt it was a long way and the only doctor at the colony might not be available. The only solution was that Lord Beresford should be transported back to Sandy Point as soon as possible to receive medical attention there. He could not remain on the pampas indefinitely.

Lord Beresford agreed that was the best thing to do. At this stage he was wishing for his bed at Huntingley and if he was delivered to the port he could take the first steamer back to England.

That evening as he relaxed, his pain temporarily dulled by a fair quantity of spirits, the course of action was agreed upon, though Thia believed it served no purpose for the rest of the party to return with him.

'Beg pardon, ma'am, but why don't I go back with his lord-ship?' Ethel said. 'Young Isaac can come along too, and one of them Indian guides can show us the way.'

Everyone was listening.

'His lordship could lodge with Señor Garcia until the ship arrives. I am sure he'd be only too happy to accommodate his lordship.'

'That sound like a splendid idea,' Lord Beresford said, his mind reviving to the thought of the four poster bed with the feather mattress. 'I might even get chance to look at those beasts after all.'

'I couldn't let you do it, Goody. I should be the one to go, not you. It's too much of a responsibility.'

'Pardon me for saying, ma'am, but I was nursemaid to both you and Mr Algernon, and Mr Horatio too, and at times that was none too easy a task. Looking after Lord Beresford will be a piece of cake.'

'Well said, Thoroughgood,' Lord Beresford added. 'As for you, dear Thia, you planned this adventure and an adventure you will have. You will not forfeit your wild dreams for the sake of a clumsy old man.'

'Oh, Papa,' she cried, hugging him carefully so as not to put pressure on his leg. 'If you will permit Goody to care for you in Sandy Point until the steamer arrives, when you board the ship there will certainly be a doctor to attend to you.'

'And I vouch you will not have a better nursemaid, Papa,' Algernon added. 'But what about your needs, Thia?'

'As Horatio pointed out before we left, there is little need for a lady's maid in the middle of the pampas. And if I am not mistaken,' she said, smiling kindly at Ethel Thoroughgood, 'you will not complain at being sent back to England early.'

Ethel smiled broadly, dropping a polite curtsy. 'I couldn't have put it better myself, ma'am.'

As usual Algernon was not sure. 'But how can we continue as if nothing is amiss when father is so indisposed?'

'My indisposition, be it here or in England, should not make the slightest difference to your expedition. You came ten thousand miles to ride across the Patagonian pampas and you may never have the opportunity to come here again. Over the last few weeks I have discovered I am a little old for this type of adventure but I have enjoyed the things I have done and seen. Now I will be happy to go back to Huntingley.'

'Thank you, Papa,' Thia said, looking at the circle of faces glowing in the flickering light of the camp-fire. 'Are we all agreed then?'

No one disagreed as everyone was quietly pleased that a decision had finally been made. There was only one thing Thia had not mentioned: with Ethel and her father no longer riding with them, there would be no one in their party to slow them down. If they rode hard and wasted no time, it was possible they would catch up with the Welshman. He was only one day's ride ahead of them.

The following morning, the plan was again discussed and Lord Beresford was adamant about the arrangements, making only one proviso. He was not going to be dragged fifty miles back to Sandy Point on the back of a litter. He was determined to ride. Making a splint delayed their departure but eventually, with his leg wrapped in fur skin encased in wooden stakes he was hoisted into the saddle for the journey back to the coast.

Thia shed a silent tear which she quickly wiped from her cheek.

'Take care of his lordship,' she said, embracing her maid, before Isaac helped her on to the side-saddle and mounted up himself. Thoroughgood was obviously happy to be heading back to Sandy Point, but Isaac could not hide his disappointment. He had relished every moment of the adventure thus far; had learned a lot of new skills and had not expected it to end so abruptly.

They were losing Jose, but he promised to catch up with them in about a week. Riding to the port with one invalid and one inexperienced rider would take several days, but once they reached the estancia, he would exchange his horse and be able to return to them with all speed.

As the group of four riders, six horses and Jose's two long-legged ostrich dogs faded into the distance, the camp was quickly dismantled and the pack horses loaded. Thia insisted they leave the shores of Lake Otway as soon as possible and make as much distance as they could before nightfall. Having given all their supplies of meat to the group returning to the town, they had only sufficient for that evening's meal.

Hopefully the next day they would cross tracks with some guanacos or ostriches. But with Jose gone, they now only had Martin and Carlos. What they ate in the next few days would depend on how accurate their aim was.

They had only been riding for an hour when a small herd of guanacos was sighted. Carlos spotted them first and though he pointed in their direction, no one could distinguish the animals in the distance. The fact their colour blended well with the landscape was one of the reasons the long necked llama-like camelids survived in great numbers on the inhospitable plains.

When they were a little closer, they all gave chase, the ostrich dogs flying off ahead with the two Newfoundlands trying to match them but unable to equal their pace. Martin and Carlos rode to either side of the herd in an attempt to force them into a knot. But the swift footed guanaco turned and scattered sending the dogs running in all directions.

By chance one of the dogs disturbed an ostrich which had been lying low, Martin gave chase spinning the *bolas* above his head and aiming them at the fleet-footed bird. The rhea doubled, changing direction far quicker than the dogs could turn, but once the *bolas* wrapped themselves around its neck and legs, it fell. Leaping from his horse, Martin quickly despatched the bird and within minutes it was hanging from his saddle. The meat would make a nice change from the waterfowl and snipe which they had been eating for the past two days.

Thia galloped on after the guanacos but was not close enough to get a shot. William who was alongside fired once. One of the guanacos stumbled, ran for a dozen yards and then fell stone dead.

121

'Well done, William,' she called, dismounting to examine his prey. 'What an excellent shot. Right through the head, and at such a distance. It must have been one hundred and fifty yards.'

'A lucky shot,' he said, laughing off her praise.

'I think not,' she said, turning to face him. 'It amazes me. I have known you for nearly three years yet in all that time I never realized you were a marksman. Why didn't you say? Algy certainly never mentioned it. Why don't you ride with the hunt?'

'I choose not to. I believe it to be a cruel pastime and I am averse to any form of blood sports – fox hunting, cock fighting, bear baiting.'

'Goodness. Then you and Mr Euan Davies are of a similar mind.'

'I was not aware of that.'

'But that does not detract from the fact that you are an excellent shot. Pray tell me, when do you go shooting?'

'Given a choice – never.'

Thia looked at him questioningly. 'But at one time you obviously did.'

'I shot an antelope when I was seven and that picture stuck in my mind. That was my first *prize*. Killing that beautiful animal was my first memory. I can still picture it now. The grass was almost as tall as me and the rifle too heavy for me to hold. My father squatted down on the ground so I could rest the barrel on his shoulder. I think it was that period of my upbringing that contributed to his later deafness.'

'You have never spoken greatly about your family.'

'No, I suppose not. My father was a colonel. He died in India when I was fourteen.'

'But didn't he wish for you to follow in his footsteps?'

'Indeed, that was always his intention. But as you see, I did not fit the mould of a soldier. I preferred painting or writing poetry and from an early age would hide away in some nook in the garden burying myself in the pages of Shakespeare or Dickens. I read anything I could lay my hands on and started writing plays at a very early age.'

'Good for you.'

He smiled, lifting the blond curl back from his forehead. 'Because I showed no interest whatsoever in military matters, Father described me as being scatterbrained and eccentric. Fortunately, my mother had always hated the prospect of me being sent to Zululand or back to India, where I had spent my early years, and later, after my father died, she was delighted when I was admitted to Cambridge.'

'And I am also delighted you chose to follow your heart as otherwise our paths would have never crossed. But we must thank your father for endowing you with the ability to put meat on our table.'

William smiled and bowed theatrically, showing a leg. 'It is my pleasure, ma'am.'

After the meal of roast ostrich, boiled guanaco head and egg custard, Thia sat quietly by the camp-fire. It was too dark to write any letters or read, and as William and Algy had already retired, she watched Martin. From a small pouch of feathers, which he took from under his bowler hat, he carefully selected a feather which he attached to the shaft of an arrow. Thia moved closer to him and asked if she might watch what he was doing. The gaucho nodded and offered her his quiver of completed arrows. She handled it carefully. She had practiced archery for several years as a girl. It was one of the few pastimes for which Horatio did not disparage her for

123

participating in. It was a sport she had enjoyed, but of latter years she had grown tired of the static target and preferred the exhilaration of riding with hounds. Yet the stories she read of the North American Indians who let fly their arrows while astride a horse still appealed to her sense of adventure.

'You not see bow on pampas today,' Martin said. 'My father teach me. I learn when boy. I like. I practise. You like?' he said, pointing to the bow.

'May I?' she said, eyeing it admiringly.

The gaucho nodded.

It was taller than she was and lighter than she had expected though she was not sure what wood it was made of. But it was strong and straight and the string was taut beneath her fingers.

'You try,' Martin said again.

'Perhaps, tomorrow,' Thia said.

CHAPTER 10

The Pampas Wind

For the next two days they spent eight hours in the saddle. The horses which they had bought from Señor Garcia were proving their worth by showing little sign of fatigue and even after fifty miles still answered the spur when called. Carlos assured them that he was following the Welshman's tracks though none of them could recognize them, so when they came upon Davies's campsite from the previous night, they were all quietly relieved. Another day and they would catch up with him.

The following morning the air was strangely still and the sun rising over the pampas particularly brilliant. The purple mountains of the Cordillera were tipped with the golden snow of morning but to the north the horizon lay under a cloud of rusty hazy. Carlos insisted they did not stop at noon, as was customary, but press on, though he did not state the reasons for the urgency. Though the companions were eager and resisted their fatigue, for the first time the horses seemed reluctant to proceed.

They were all delighted when they saw a rider approaching and discovered it was Euan. But he was alone, was whipping his horse and riding at a full gallop. As he drew closer they could see he was shouting but were unable to understand what he was calling. But his cry appeared urgent and he was turning in the saddle and pointing back towards the mountains.

The looming cloud was following him and heading straight for them. It was rolling across the pampas like a tidal wave.

'Cover your faces!' Davies shouted, as he rode past heading back to help the two gauchos throw lead ropes over the pack animals. A wild pampas wind had the power to drive loose horses fifty miles from where they had been travelling.

'A few miles ahead,' he shouted. 'There is a house. You must ride quickly.'

At Davies's insistence, everyone led one of the pack horses while he led two and Carlos and Martin another pair each. Unable to gallop towing an unwilling horse, they cantered on heading straight into the swirling cloud which was taller than any cliff.

When the face of the storm hit, it roared across them with the noise of a steam train, pelting their faces with dust and fine stones and almost dislodging them from their saddles. Closing their eyes to the onslaught they lost sight of each other. The horses shied and had to be spurred on, their pace reduced to a walk. Voices called out but the sounds were quickly carried away.

It took only five minutes for the worst of the sandstorm to roll over them leaving only a strong wind blowing in its wake. As it calmed, the air became breathable and clear enough for them to see how easily it had disorganized the group. Remarkably Thia had managed to stay close beside

William while Algernon had dropped well behind. Martin had separated. He had gone looking for three of the pack horses which had broken from the line and were out of sight.

'Keep close,' Davies shouted, encouraging them to go on despite the battering both horse and rider were still receiving.

The small farmhouse was less than a mile distant though until they reached its fenced corral they had been unable to see it. It was a modest, stone-built house, quite different to the wood and iron huts of Punta Arenas but lowly in comparison with the house on the estancia. Painted white, it had a dark shingle roof and a stout square chimney. A picket fence enclosed a cottage garden which was sheltered by a row of six year old poplar trees.

The Indian woman was waiting for them in the corral. Once the gate was locked and the horses unsaddled, they hurried for the shelter of the house. Thia found the door wide open and knocked but no one answered.

Inside the two-roomed house the furnishings were simple – hand-hewn wooden table and chairs and bed. But the addition of a few simple ornaments and pictures gave the house a homely feeling.

When Davies came in from the yard, his expression was grave.

'You are lucky this place is here,' he said. 'The wind can be merciless.' He did not touch anything but he walked through the two-roomed house observing how it had been left.

'Who lives here?' Thia asked.

'Helmut Lechter and his wife. He is Austrian.'

'Have they run from the wind?'

'Why would they? This is the best place to be in such a blow.'

Thia took off her hat and rubbed the grit from her eyes.

127

'What brought you here?'

'Last night I saw the smoke from your camp-fire and again this morning and knew you were not far behind. When I saw the change in the sky, I knew what to expect. I also knew that the wind would drive off your spare horses and you would be in trouble.'

'Thank you for coming back.'

Davies nodded as he brushed the dust from his trousers.

'When the wind drops, I will help you search. I believe some of your baggage-horses may also be missing. For now, I suggest you light a fire and eat a meal.'

'But what of the farmer?'

'Helmut and Frau Lechter would make you welcome. If you wish when you leave, you can thank them for their hospitality. You can leave a box of cartridges, a tin of coffee or bag of sugar. Not money, though. He is a proud man.'

Thia examined the table. The tin plates from the last meal were still set out on it and a jug of milk had been placed in the centre. She picked it up and swirled it about. But the milk was curdled.

'It looks like they left in a hurry.'

Davies didn't comment. 'I suggest you stay here for the night.'

With a fire lit and a fresh pot of meat stewing in the iron pot, the party settled around the fire. Outside the wind had not yet blown itself out and at times it returned the fire smoke into the room.

Wandering around the small room, Thia studied a framed picture on the wall. The handsome woman, standing beside her husband in a pleasant parlour looked out of place in the wilds of the Patagonian pampas.

'What do they do here?'

'They are sheep farmers and they have three children,' Davies said.

Thia looked at the child's cot in the corner near the fireplace. It had been stripped of its blankets.

'But what of the sheep?' Algernon asked. 'We jumped no fences.'

'Unlike the farms you have in the English counties, the sheep range over hundreds of miles. They're as hardy as the black-faced sheep on the windswept Pennines. They do not know what a fence is.'

'And sheep are your business you say.'

'Yes.'

'And you are heading to your farm?' William asked.

'No. My land is on Tierra del Fuego. I have about two thousand sheep there.'

Algernon was impressed. 'Welsh sheep?'

'No, sir, most came from the Falkland Islands and I imported some from New Zealand.'

'Fancy that.'

'Mr Davies,' Thia said, 'in your opinion, why would the family have left in such a hurry?'

'Maybe there was an accident or one of the children was ill. There is a good doctor in Sandy Point. However, it is more likely they were warned of danger and left before it reached them.'

'You mean the wind?'

'No, they left well before that.'

'Then why? What danger?' Thia asked anxiously, looking at the rifled cupboards and broken dresser drawers.

'Indians?' Algernon asked.

At first Davies seemed reluctant to answer. 'Not full-blood Tehuelche Indians. It is not their nature,' he said. 'Wild cowboys sometimes travel down from North America. Sometimes convicts escape from the Sandy Point prison, steal horses and anything else they need and then find there are few places to run to. There is nothing for them on Tierra del Fuego and there is nothing to the west but sea channels, and frozen ice. That leaves the north and east. Port Saint Julian is a popular port where anyone can get a boat to Buenos Ayres or Monte Video where no one will ask questions. From there they can head north to Bolivia or Mexico or North America, or take a ship if they can find the money. They would be foolish to stay in Patagonia.'

'And what of the Cordillera? Would they try to cross it?'

'At certain times of the year. Like now – mid summer, it is possible. Martin will tell you when he comes back. He has crossed several times. There are a few passes through the high mountains but the journey is long and hard and one needs a guide and plenty of good horses. Alternatively they could ride north but they would have several swollen rivers to cross.'

'But will such men find anything on the pampas?' Thia asked.

'Very little. On the pampas there is only a handful of estancias and hardly any farmhouses such as this. There are scattered groups of Indians, but they are nomadic. But travellers like yourselves are almost unknown.'

'And towns?'

'There is the Welsh settlement at Rawson on the Chubut River, but it is poor despite the effort of the farmers. It is a peaceful farming community. I know it well; I grew up there. The folk there are strong-willed and united and a convict would soon end up with a noose around his neck if he ventured into the town intent on stealing or worse.'

'If it was escaped convicts which made Herr Lechter leave his home, is it likely they will come back?'

'I don't think so.'

'Did you hear of any convicts escaping the gaol when we were in town?'

'No.'

After a hearty meal spiced with home-made German mustards and peppers from Frau Lechter's pantry, William was bullied into reciting some of his poetry. He was accompanied by the wind humming through the eaves and whistling down the chimney. As there were few chairs, Thia sat on the floor between her two dogs. She had been frantic when they had disappeared in the storm, though Davies had assured her they would find their own way to the house. What relief it was when they barked outside the door. Thia promised herself that from then on she would not let them out of her sight.

They were mid-way through a game of charades when everyone noticed a sudden stillness. Trooping outside, they found that the wind had died completely and there was not a cloud in the sky. In the moon's orange glow, nothing appeared different, though on closer inspection the wind had flogged the earth stripping every particle of dust from its hard surface. Despite the fact the horses had not eaten, it was decided to keep them corralled all night as a precaution against a storm springing up again.

The next morning Davies was concerned. Martin had still not returned. He was hopeful the Peruvian guide had located some of the horses, particularly the pack-horses which had run off. If so, he would have tethered them and camped on the pampas overnight and would be returning with them at first light.

But the next day arrived and still there was no sign of the gaucho. The missing baggage-horses carried the tents and some of the provisions and unless they could be found, a return to Sandy Point would be necessary. Davies explained the situation and the alternatives.

'We will wait a little longer,' he said. 'We do not know how far he has had to ride.'

'You take life very seriously,' Thia said later when the Welshman was standing outside gazing at the horizon.

'And do you take it lightly?'

There was something about him which intrigued and puzzled her. She found him very hard to fathom.

'Did Herr Lechter leave suddenly because he was attacked?'

'No, but I think he left because the Indians warned him of the danger.'

'Danger? Who from?'

'Evil men bent on reeking more evil.'

'And does the pampas attract such men?'

'Not the pampas, but Sandy Point. I told you the population grew from seamen heaved from sailing ships, crazed men left to die; from sealers and whalers who came into town to drink away their wages. Now the town is beset with gold fever attracting those who want to make a quick fortune, but have no intention of making the town their home. And there are itinerants who drift down from the north. They kill the sheep to eat so the farmers who have struggled to settle the land turn to bullets to protect their property.'

'What of the natives of Patagonia?'

'The Tehuelche Indians are being pushed from the pampas. They are a peace-loving people. They die mainly from the diseases the white man brings.'

'Do they kill their enemies?'

'Yes, if they are attacked and have to defend themselves. And sometimes they seek retribution.' He paused for a moment. 'But, in this part of the world, mostly nature takes care of their enemies. White men cannot survive here. They die from starvation. Those who steal boats and sail west from Sandy Point head into the uncharted channels which weave between thousands of tiny islands. Most of the coastline is impenetrable. Where there is no vegetation there is sheer rock or glaciers – and there are many of those. Many foolish white men have become hopelessly lost and perished.'

'You will stay with us, won't you?' Thia said.

'I shall ride with you to the foothills of the Cordillera. From there I will head to the high passes and you will return to Punta Arenas for your steamer. Carlos and Martin will guide you back. Today I will go hunting with Carlos. You and your friends will stay here while the horses are allowed out to graze.'

'Will we ride again tomorrow?'

'That depends. If Martin does not return by tomorrow morning, I will go and search for him.'

CHAPTER 11

Martin

The sound of horses approaching woke them early. Thia quickly pulled on her clothes and reached for her rifle but before she got outside she could hear laughter and recognized the excited tones of the young Huntingley groom. Isaac and Jose had ridden almost non-stop to catch up with the group after delivering Lord Beresford to the estancia of Señor Garcia at Punta Arenas.

'His lordship said I'd be more use here than sitting around waiting for the next steamer,' Isaac said, his smile stretching from ear to ear.

'And how is my father,' Thia asked.

'His lordship's fine, ma'am. Mrs Thoroughgood says the swelling in his leg had gone down and to tell you that there is a ferry arrives for them on the thirtieth.'

'And how did Jose find us? Surely the wind blew all the tracks away.'

'Aye, sir, it did. But Mr Jose was certain that we would find you here at the house.'

'Well, I am sure we are all pleased to see you, Isaac.'

'Thank you, ma'am. I'm sure pleased to be back with you.'

The mood over breakfast was cheerful. Isaac was quizzed about the journey to the coast which he described in as much detail as he could remember. He said they had travelled at a reasonable pace and apart from Mrs Thoroughgood being alarmed by the incessant purring of a puma during the night, nothing eventful had happened.

Thia and her brother were relieved to know that Lord Beresford was now in the safe hands of Señor Garcia and in a week's time would be on a ship back to England.

From the window, Thia noticed that Davies was saddling his horse and went out to enquire where he was going. 'Martin should have come back either with the horses or to report that he could not find them. As Jose saw no signs of him, I must go and look for him. Carlos will stay here with you.'

'I would like to ride with you,' Thia said.

'I ride fast and may be in the saddle for many hours.'

'I promise I will not slow you down.'

Surprised when he agreed that she could accompany him, Thia ran inside to collect her hat, gloves and rifle. By this time, Carlos had rounded up some of the horses and brought them back to the corral. Within minutes he had the *lazo* around the neck of one of the mares and it was standing quietly.

Isaac was anxious to help and although Thia assured him she could manage on her own, she was glad of his assistance. She did not want to keep the Welshman waiting.

'Look after my dogs,' she cried to the lad, as she leapt up into the saddle and, after briefly farewelling the others, the pair headed in the direction the pampas wind had been blowing. It was likely the pack-horses had tried to outrun the wind

135

and in doing so had been carried along with it until it ran out of strength or the horses stumbled or exhausted themselves.

Riding into the morning sun was not easy. Davies wore a broad brimmed felt hat which fastened under the chin, but Thia's hat gave her eyes little protection from the glare but she did not complain.

As the hours wore on, the sun lifted in the sky and warmed the prairie.

Whenever Thia glanced at her riding companion, his eyes were scanning the ground.

'Are there tracks?' she asked.

'No. The ground is rock hard and the topsoil has been stripped away. Hopefully we will find something further along. If Martin stopped for the night he would have built a fire and may have left it burning so we would see the smoke.'

'But how do you know which way to go?'

'I don't. It is likely the horses headed back to the place they last grazed. Or perhaps they returned to Sandy Point. It's possible Martin has followed them all the way back to the coast.'

'But that is at least two days from here.'

'Indeed.'

He spurred his horse to a gallop and they rode on in silence. A rat-like creature darted down a hole in the ground. The fox it was fleeing from was not more than twenty yards away.

'*Tucu-tucu,*' Euan said, pointing to the rodent.

The fox stopped in its tracks. It was a large grey-brown predator with a patchy coat which lacked any sheen. It looked at them scornfully for a moment before turning and slinking away.

They pair rode on. Behind them were the mountain ranges.

Ahead the pampas stretched endlessly with no sign of life, neither man nor horse.

It was midday when they stopped briefly to rest the horses and eat a biscuit.

'You are a very private man, Mr Davies,' Thia said, as she dismounted.

'Yes, ma'am.'

'Please call me Thia. My name is Cynthia, but I prefer not to be called that. And I shall call you Euan, if I may?'

He did not object.

'You have a Welsh name and you speak with traces of a Welsh accent. Will you tell me where your home is?'

'My rightful home is here under the Patagonian sky. There is no other place on earth quite like it – a vast emptiness you can call your own. Perhaps the sea is a close alternative, but then there are usually other people around you.' He looked across at her. 'But that is not the answer you wanted to hear, is it?'

She shook her head.

'When I am not in South America, I live in Liverpool. I was born in South Wales but have very little memory of it. My parents were amongst the first settlers in the Chubut Valley, north from here. They sailed to Argentina in 1865 on *Mimosa* and built a town called Rawson. That is where I grew up. Everyone who lives there is Welsh and that is the language they speak.'

'How odd – a Welsh town in the middle of South America.'

'That is where I learned to ride. That is where I first saw the gauchos. As boy I admired their skill on a horse and with the *bolas* and wanted to be like them. Rawson was my home until my parents were drowned when the Chubut River flooded. Then I was shipped back to Wales to live with an old uncle

137

and though he had some land and a horse for me to ride, I always wanted to return to South America. When my uncle died, I inherited enough money to do that.'

'Did you go back to the Welsh settlement?'

'No. The country is poor and the farmers struggle for survival. I sailed to Buenos Ayres and from there to Punta Arenas – Sandy Point as the English call it. Land was cheap on Tierra del Fuego so I bought my first farm and imported sheep. I come back here every spring.'

'Were you ever married?'

'For a short time.'

'And your wife?'

'She is dead.'

Thia paused. Gazing into the distance she saw nothing remarkable, only miles of treeless prairie which appeared flat.

'William is intrigued by the Indian woman who is travelling with us. Will you tell me a little about her?'

He breathed deeply before replying. 'Her name is Ana. She is a full-blood Tehuelche Indian.'

'May I ask why she is travelling with us?'

'It is her choice.'

As he spoke his attention was attracted to something he could see in the distance.

'What is it?' Thia asked.

'Quick!' he said. 'There is no time to waste.'

Unable to see any movement or even dust on the open pampas and not knowing what was up ahead, Thia leapt into her saddle and rode off at a rapid pace in pursuit of the Welshman. Spurring their horses they rode hard for half an hour till Davies abruptly reined in his horse. Thia instantly recognized the items strewn across the ground around them – the contents of one of their canvas baggage packs. Twenty yards away was a pile of poles, tarpaulins and guanaco skins.

'What happened here? Where is the horse?'

'The pack might have slipped and tangled around its legs. It would have kicked until the girth broke.'

'Shall we gather these things together and take them back?'

Davies did not answer. He was not interested in the damaged pots and scattered provisions. His eyes were on the vultures wheeling in the sky only a mile further ahead. Without speaking he spurred his horse.

When Thia caught up to him, he turned in his saddle.

'It is best you wait here.'

'Why?'

'Wait here,' he said abruptly, riding off.

Thia waited, considering the worst. If the horse's legs were still entangled in ropes or leather thongs, it was likely it had been brought down and the vultures were waiting for it to die. She waited expecting to hear a rifle shot, but none rang out.

Dismounting, she walked slowly in the direction Euan had ridden.

Beside a cold fireplace, she found him kneeling on the ground. In front of him the remains of a man's body was staked out on the ground. Though he had been stripped of his poncho and bowler hat, she instantly recognized the layers of leather on Martin's high-heeled boots.

'God rest his soul,' she said, her heart thumping.

Euan Davies got up, took her hands and led her away.

But the scene was already imprinted in her mind. The man's arms and legs drawn out, his wrists and ankles tied to four of Huntingley's tent pegs driven into the ground. Nothing of his face remained recognizable and his stomach had been ripped open by the vultures. But a strip of guanaco skin wound tightly around his neck was still evident.

'What evil creature did this?'

The Welshman did not answer.

'Tell me he died before the vultures got to him.'

'I can't,' he said. 'That strip of fresh skin wound around his neck would have strangled him slowly as it dried. The night air would have chilled him half to death. But the vultures would not have refused a carcass which did not have the strength to fight back.'

Thia shuddered. 'But what makes men do this sort of thing?'

'Because they are evil. They do this for their own amusement.'

'But Martin was so kind. He would hurt no one. He always had a smile on his face.' Thia looked around at the remains of the campsite and the contents of the canvas packs. 'What do you think happened here?' she asked.

'Martin had obviously found the run-away horses. He would have tethered them when he made camp for the night. The men who killed him must have surprised him when he was sleeping. I know he would not have surrendered easily so it is likely they shot him first. Let us hope so.'

'But what did they want from him?'

'The horses of course. And now they have three at least.'

'Do you know of these men?' she asked quizzically.

He thought for a moment before answering. 'I heard in Sandy Point that a shopkeeper had been killed and his wife raped. His house was ransacked and his guns and rifles stolen. Then an Indian was killed and his horses stolen. I believe the same men were responsible.'

'But you did not tell us about these things.'

'It was not your problem.'

'Now they have killed one of our guides, I think it is!' She paused. 'What do we do now?'

'Gather the things you can find into a pile. I will ask Jose and Carlos to come back here with the spare horses to collect them. I will take Martin. We cannot bury him here and there is no firewood to burn his body.'

The vultures, sitting no more than five paces away, were becoming impatient craning their ugly bare necks and extending their wings at the pair of unwelcome intruders. In a fit of anger Thia ran at them waving her arms wildly and screaming at the top of her voice. The birds squawked and lifted themselves a few yards off the ground, hovered for a few moments before swooping back and settling on the ground a little further away.

'You will not deter them,' Davies said, pointing to the sky. The black spots dotting the sky had drawn him to this place. The big birds were still resting effortlessly on the currents of warm air and appeared not to be moving. There were plenty of scavengers waiting for a feed.

Wasting no time, Davies pulled the knife from his belt and cut the taut leather ties from Martin's wrists and ankles. Rolling the Peruvian's corpse in his own *capa*, he laid the body over the horse. As it would be necessary to walk the horses to the isolated farmhouse, they both knew it would be dark before they got back.

Using all the firewood they had carried with them, the motley group cremated Martin's body in the hour before dawn, sending a broad plume of black smoke into the breaking sky. Davies and the gauchos knew that the distinctive column rising from the funeral pyre would be a beacon for miles around. It was unlike the smoke from a camp-fire or a hearth and any Indian would read what it was and would know exactly where it was coming from.

Lying in bed, Thia's body ached with tiredness, but she could not sleep. Her mind was awash with the scene of horror she had witnessed and the knowledge that the men who had done it were somewhere out on the pampas.

'If you take my advice, you will return to Sandy Point,' Davies said. 'Jose and Carlos will accompany you. If you insist on an excursion over the pampas, then I suggest you take the local schooner to Port Saint Julian. From there you can ride north – all the way to Buenos Ayres if you wish.'

'Will you come with us?'

'No. There are things I must do.'

Thia looked to Algy and William for confirmation. 'Then we will go on, with you. We discussed that very question last night. We came here to ride to the Cordillera and now we are very close, we do not want to turn back. We also feel it would not be safe for you to travel alone. Including yourself and Ana, there are eight of us. We can all ride fast and shoot straight and defend ourselves if attacked. We are not afraid.'

'The pampas can be a dangerous place.'

'Because of the men who murdered Martin?'

'Yes.'

'Do you know who they are, or where they came from?'

'They escaped from prison.'

'But you said that no one had escaped from the gaol at Sandy Point.'

'I did not lie. They came from the north.'

Thia looked puzzled. 'Do you know which way they will ride?'

'They will not return to Sandy Point, I can vouch for that.

And they will not go east as the rivers are too broad to cross further downstream. I think they are heading north-west in the hope of crossing the Cordillera.'

'Do you think we will cross tracks with them again?'

Davies shrugged. 'They will be travelling fast and carrying few supplies. They will only stop to catch and eat what they need on the way.'

'Or steal it?'

'Yes. But there are no more houses or estancias ahead and no Indian camps. They never stay in one place for long. Besides, I think the natives already know of these men. It was probably the Indians who warned Herr Lechter to leave in such a hurry.' He thought for a moment. 'Today we must hunt. There are guanaco in this region and rhea. We will spend one more night here and then move on.'

With additional packs filled with meat and skins and the gauchos' saddle-packs loaded with bundles of ostrich feathers, they rode away from the Lechters' cottage wondering when the farmer would return and hoping that the ashes from the pyre would blow away in the next wind.

At last they were riding towards the Cordillera whose high snow-capped peaks were strikingly rugged against the spotless sky. The bare plateau ended abruptly at the foothills which were clothed in a curtain of green. The thick forests stretched almost to the snowline.

'Will you tell me a little about your wife, Euan? Was she as handsome as Ana?'

'She was very similar in looks. They were sisters.'

CHAPTER 12

The Ravine

Ahead in the distance was what appeared to be an immense long lake, shining silvery white in the early morning rays and snaking far into the distance towards the high mountains. They rode towards it, but, as the sun grew in the sky and the air warmed the earth, the illusive white lake dissolved into thin air, revealing a broad ravine hidden beneath it. The steep sides, almost perpendicular in parts, dropped over 300 feet below them. Stretching roughly north to south, the ravine formed a seemingly impossible barrier to cross, but, as the valley swept away into the distance, they could see a track. It zigzagged all the way down to the river bounded on one side by a strip of lush green.

'We must descend and cross this river,' Davies said. 'The way is treacherous, so be extra careful. A fall could be fatal. When we reach the bottom we will follow the river upstream until we can find a safe place to ford.'

Forming a single file the riders followed the Welshman along the edge of the ravine and on to a rough track hewn by the wild horses. As the path descended it crossed a slurry of shale held loosely in place by inhospitable thorn bushes and tufts of stunted grass. It looked impassable but Davies insisted it was used regularly by the Indians.

As they left the safety of the plateau and rode down into the shadow of the sun, the ravine grew grey and gloomy. But as the sun lifted it dismissed the lingering mist and the contours of the valley were laid out before them.

It was a broad canyon which wound its way unchanging into the distance. At the bottom, the icy glacial melt-water spawned in the high Andes, rumbled between sheer rock walls cutting the valley deeper and projecting its full force against any fallen boulders. Early summer meant that the snow fields of the Cordillera had already succumbed to the spring thaw and the worst was past. Now the river was slowing and in a few weeks time the amount of water would be reduced to a quarter of its present volume.

No one spoke as they rode on, the horses knuckling at times. Loose rocks, dislodged from beneath their hoofs, were sent showering down the precipitous side, picking up an avalanche of small stones on the way. Each time a horse regained its stride, the rider's heart returned to a steady beat.

As the ravine curved broadly to the right, the sides became less steep,though the path narrowed. They had been descending slowly but were less than halfway down when a rat ran in front of William's mount. Tossing its head back, the horse lost its footing.

William struggled to stay seated. He was fully aware of the consequences if the horse tumbled sideways. Wrenching its head around, he turned his mount to face the river below. His only chance was to ride the scree to the bottom of the ravine. Leaning back across the horse's rump, he braced his legs, gripped tightly and, like a man at the reins of a toboggan, let the horse slide. There was nothing to stop them. The loose shale was as slippery as a snowfield. Gaining speed, the horse made a futile effort to regain its stride, its hoofs clattering noisily through the shower of stones. As horse and rider descended they were engulfed in a cloud of dust.

Two hundred feet below the level of the pampas, the river's powerful current had eroded the hard rock, and created a channel of deep water on the eastern side. The grassy bank was on the opposite side. When horse and rider slid into the river they disappeared beneath its fast moving flow.

Watching from above, William's companions were frantic, but they could do nothing. They could neither turn in their tracks nor dismount and any hope of climbing down the slope was out of the question.

The dogs however were alert to the tragedy the moment it unfolded. All six scrambled down the shale slithering on their bellies. As was to be expected, the ostrich dogs reached the bottom first. With the legs of a greyhound, they were built for speed and agility and were familiar with this type of terrain. Yapping continually, they bounded along the rocks keeping pace with the man and horse that were now being tossed about in the churning water. At times the horse made contact with the rocky bottom and kicked in an effort to reclaim its feet but the current was too strong and washed it off balance.

William was struggling to unfasten the rifle strapped across his shoulder and, as he entered a whirlpool, the water curled over his head and he was dragged under.

The dogs watched him disappear and barked continuously but made no effort to jump in.

'Get him, Bella! Go, Byron!' Thia screamed, the echo of her voice bouncing back and forth across the valley walls.

The pair of Huntingley dogs was at the bottom of the
ravine only seconds behind the gauchos' dogs, but being
Newfoundlands, they immediately plunged into the freezing
flow. With their heavy coats insulating them from the cold
and a cushion of air trapped in their thick undercoat buoying
them up, they drifted downstream paddling defiantly. On
reaching the drowning man they both pushed their heads
beneath his arms and supported him. With one dog on either
side of him, William ceased struggling, relaxed and allowed
the pair to deliver him to safety. They were swept along till
the river turned and the current veered to the opposite side
where William and the two Newfoundlands were washed up
on a pebbly beach. They had travelled almost half a mile
downstream.

From their vantage point the party cheered as they saw
their friend emerge from the water, stagger on to the beach
and wave weakly. Beside him the dogs were shaking themselves vigorously, showering the man in a spray of cold water,
but by now he appeared oblivious to his rescuers. The fact he
had survived both the fall and the river's turbulence, relieved
and delighted his companions. For the present the sun was
streaming down on the far side of the valley. It would help to
warm him. Their main concern now was how to reach him.

They had no choice but to continue down the narrow winding path aware that at any minute any one of them could slip
with similar dire consequences. Following in single file with
the stream of spare horses following them, it took over an
hour for the party to complete their tedious descent. Once
they reached the bottom they had to ride upstream for quite a
distance to find a suitable place to ford. Then they had to
track back along the river-bank at far side – a total distance of
about two miles. As they rounded each turn in the river they

expected to find the small beach which William had been washed up on and, after a time, began to despair of ever reaching the place where he had fallen.

Eventually they found him, sitting on a pebbled beach, his arms around the two Newfoundlands. Davies nodded to him, satisfying himself the man was all right, then continued along the bank heading downstream. He hoped the horse may also have made it to safety.

'William! William! Praise the Lord!' Algernon cried, leaping from his mount. 'I feared I had lost you!' Unable to embrace his seated friend he patted him on the head in a paternal fashion, shaking his head at the same time.

'Not yet, Algy, and certainly not to a river. In time you may lose me to a woman whose soul is as deep as this stretch of river and whose spirit is as free as the pampas.'

'Forever the poet,' Algernon said.

'Whatever fate lies ahead, I promise you, my dear friend, you will never lose my friendship. And tell me, how could I possibly desert you when there are so many lessons I must still teach you?' William smiled his sweetest smile while Algernon's eyes glistened in the sunlight.

'Enough of your jokes, William,' Thia said, 'you are cold. You must get out of those wet clothes. Come let me help you.'

As she unbuttoned his jacket and shirt and struggled to peel the clinging garments from him, Ana slid the *capa* from her shoulders.

'Take,' she said. 'Be warm.'

'I cannot,' he said, gazing into her dark fathomless eyes.

'Take,' she said, pressing the fur skin into his hands. Then she turned and began collecting pieces of driftwood washed downstream from the beechwood forests.

With a fire burning on the beach, food, hot chocolate and a

set of dry clothing, William soon regained full control of his limbs. After an hour's rest he was able to remount a fresh horse. Davies had found William's horse a mile further downstream. Grazing contentedly on a bank of soft grass, it appeared none the worse for its tumble. Leading it back he reminded the party of the incredible hardiness of the Criollo horses. With no blanket to warm it, he put his faith in the sun and the fact that the horse had been able to graze for over an hour. As the ravine on this side of the valley was far less steep than the one they had traversed, he assured them that if the horse was fit enough, it would follow them.

The party made camp a little further upstream close to the ford where they had crossed. Here the bank was soft and the river offered the opportunity to bathe in the shallows. Thia was happy to swim there even though the water was very cold.

As she emerged from her tent dressed in fresh clothing, her skin tingled and her face glowed but William's accident troubled her.

If he had not managed to stay seated, he would have been lost. She could not bear to think about it.

'He is like family to us,' Thia said.

'Like a brother to me,' Algy said. 'Such a different character to Horatio. But are you not aware of William's fondness for you?'

Thia looked puzzled. 'I love him dearly and regard him with the affection of a brother.'

'I think his feelings for you could be deeper than that,' her brother added. 'I presume he has never said anything.'

Thia laughed and made light of the suggestion. 'You cannot be correct.'

149

'It is true. William has told me more than once how much he admires you, and I watch the way his eyes follow you at times.'

'But I watch the way his eyes follow Ana, the Indian. He watches her all the time. She is like a magnet to his gaze.'

'An artist's eye. An inquisitive eye,' Algernon said. 'He watches her as he would a bird or a cloud or a leaf. He sees beauty in everything. My dear Cynthia, you must realize you are a very eligible woman, a little outspoken perhaps, but intelligent, courageous, and of excellent breeding.'

'You make me sound like a horse!'

'You would make William an excellent wife.'

'Please, Algy, stop that. You sound just like Horatio telling me who I should marry. That will never do. But what about you, Algy?'

Algernon shrugged.

Thia studied her brother for a moment. 'You will make some lady an excellent husband.'

'I cannot imagine any woman would want me.'

'And why not? You are adorable and soft and gentle just like Papa. But I will offer you one piece of advice and charge you nothing for it.'

'And what is that?'

'Do not choose an independent and pig-headed girl like me, for your bride. It is enough having one such stubborn article in the family. Huntingley could never cope with two.'

Early the following morning the camp was woken to a rumbling sound echoing along the valley. Was it an earthquake? Running from her tent to join the others, Thia feared a landslide could send the loose scree tumbling down on them. What confronted the friends however was a rising cloud of dust sweeping down the valley from beyond the next bend in the river. Was it another sandstorm caught in the ravine, or even worse, a flood of water roaring down from the Andes stripping everything in its path?

Then she saw them – hundreds of horses splashing across the river. They never stopped to drink but galloped across as though the hounds of hell were at their heels. Once on the other side they pushed and kicked to gain right of way along the steep path leading up the side of the ravine.

Hearing the snorting and neighing from their own horses, Thia turned – alarmed that their mounts would try to follow. But Davies and the gauchos had already made certain none would attempt to join the wild bunch. Within minutes the mob was stretched nose to tail along the winding path creating an avalanche of small boulders which tumbled down the steep side and slashed into the water.

Ten minutes after they had made their presence felt, the pack was gone and the dust had settled over the valley. It was time to move on.

From the ravine they emerged to another plateau slightly higher than the one they had left. It stretched for several miles ending at the foothills of the mountains. As they neared the first ridge, pockets of beechwood trees began dotting the landscape. After being on the flat for so long, they were at last entering a different landscape. They all welcomed the change.

Beyond the wooded hill, the blue outline of the mountains rose sharply. Unlike pictures of any mountain Thia had ever seen before, the peaks were angular and serrated like an old saw, some of its teeth pointed and sharp, others broken and irregular. Uninviting and dangerous.

Immediately ahead of them was a large lake and a column

of smoke was rising from a grove of beechwood not far away. Davies was wary. The party halted and took out their rifles as a precaution. Skirting to the far side of the trees, he rode ahead to investigate.

The Indian told him they had been camped there for a week. There was plenty of wildfowl on the water and the natives had killed a wild stallion which would provide them with meat for several days and with leather which the women could make into goods to trade at Sandy Point.

The camp consisted of several conical shaped dwellings supported by poles, but in place of canvas each roof was covered in dozens of guanaco skins stitched together. In all, the tents housed about fifty Tehuelche Indians. Their horses, which represented their wealth were grazing on the grassy area around the lake's edge. They had a mob of about 200.

Most of the men were sitting in front of the tents smoking pipes while the women were weaving the fillets with which they tied their hair. One was sewing a boot made from a horse's hock.

Davies, Ana and one of the guides dismounted and were greeted by the Indians. The smiling faces were infectious prompting the others to dismount. The Indians were friendly and welcomed them. Thia was surprised that most spoke some English and Spanish as well as their own language.

Like Ana, the women were tall, almost six feet tall and the men slightly taller. They were a happy race, their white teeth shining from their hairless faces. The *cacique* said they had been following the wild herd since the stallion they killed had stolen several of their mares. But they had had no success in retrieving all their horses and feared they might lose more if the wild herd returned. For the present they had decided to give up the chase. This area of the plateau was well supplied with ostriches, so they had taken advantage of the hunting. Beside the tents, bundles of ostrich feathers were piled high ready for transport to the trading post at Sandy Point.

That evening they shared a meal with the Indians feasting on ostrich roasted over an open fire supplemented with ostrich pâté and the red carafate berries which the women had collected from the pampas. The Indians were pleased to receive the bag of sugar which the travellers gave them.

After the meal, Thia watched the women weaving and the men making *bolas* from stones and strips of leather.

As the maté was passed around, Davies asked if they had seen any other men on the pampas.

The *cacique* said the previous day they had seen smoke at the far side of the ravine. To Davies, that meant the men he was following had not yet crossed the river, but as it wound to the south they would have to cross it soon or they would find themselves heading back in the direction of the coast.

The next morning they left the Indian encampment early though not before their hosts had already gone off hunting.

Now they were heading west with the elusive mountain peaks at last appearing a little closer. They were leaving the plateaux behind and ahead the rolling hills rose fairly rapidly under a cover of green.

At first the pockets of beechwood grew in scattered clumps but soon the woods became denser and impenetrable. Riding through the thickets, they were again limited to single file, the brushwood tearing at their legs and scratching the horses' flanks. This was the domain of the wild horse, the fox, the pumas and mountain lions and once on the narrow tracks there was no turning around or going back. As they rode higher, the trees blocked out the sun and the forest path took on a quiet gloom.

Thia was pleased when they emerged into a broad open clearing with yet another plateau stretching ahead. Davies suggested they make camp on the edge of the trees and make use of the rest of the afternoon by hunting the herds of guanacos that were grazing on the plain.

Feeling heavy in the stomach, Thia decided not to ride with them; instead she offered to help Isaac setting up the tents.

By now she was adept at unpacking the baggage-horses and assembling the tents and a kitchen. Isaac was a willing worker and needed no prompting. After unsaddling her horse she carried it into her tent. The blankets and leather sheet which went under the saddle made an excellent mattress providing protection from the cold and damp of the earth at night. The saddle was her pillow, the skins she sat on, her blanket.

'Will you be all right on your own,' William asked, as they prepared to ride away.

'Of course,' Thia replied adamantly, hiding the slight tinge of embarrassment she felt after the revelation her brother had made to her about the way her friend regarded her. 'Those dreadful men are far from here and I shall not be alone. Isaac is here, and I shall keep Byron with me,' she said.

CHAPTER 13

Byron

It was a pretty camp, in amongst a grove of beechwood trees. It resembled a glade in a forest in England though the under-growth was as coarse as highland heather. Glancing skywards Thia saw a pair of condors circling the sky. She thought of the vultures and quickly remembered where she was.

'Can I get you anything, ma'am?' Isaac asked, as he broke up a pile of twigs and branches which he had dragged into the camp – kindling for the evening's fire.

'They are large birds,' Thia said, gazing skyward.

'So I've heard, ma'am. Mr Davies said that if you laid two of the Tehuelche Indians on the ground, head to foot, they would equal the span of a condor's wings – about twelve feet across.'

'Extraordinary. He had not told me that.'

Thia thought about the black feather Davies carried concealed beneath his shirt. What was its significance? She had also seen some natives on the street in Sandy Point and noted the feathers which decorated their spears. She wondered if those feathers also came from the great Andean Condor.

When Isaac went off to gather more wood, Thia was left alone but did not feel lonely. Byron was with her. She busied herself tiding the tents, shaking the skins or hanging them in the sun to refresh them. She was longing for a bath. It was the one thing she missed while she was travelling. She resolved to bathe in the next lake or river they came to even if the water was freezing cold.

As she laid the kindling for the fire, her father's dog nuzzled under her arm. Byron had not wanted to stay and had whined when Bella had gone hunting with the riders and other dogs. But once they were out of sight and he was alone with his mistress, the Newfoundland was content to lie in the sun. After a while, his long shaggy overcoat absorbed the heat and he sidled into the shade beside one of the tents.

Having unpacked the iron pot and crockery Thia wandered around the camp picking up more small twigs to use as kindling. Isaac would be back soon with larger branches for the evening's fire.

For a while she examined Martin's long bow but the indelible memory of what had happened to him came streaming back. Leaning the bow and quiver against the tent, she wondered what would become of those items. She would like to be able to take them back to England but did not know if Martin had a wife in Sandy Point or in Peru, the country he had come from. When Euan Davies returned she would ask him.

A noise in the brushwood startled her. She looked over to Byron. He had heard it too. His short ears were pricked to the sound. Her heart raced for fear it was the men who had killed

Martin. She listened but everything was silent. A guanaco or ostrich in the bushes? A fox perhaps? Or one of their own horses forcing its way through the undergrowth? She waited for a moment – listening. There it was again – the crack of a twig. Her mind flashed to the Indians. They were not far away. But they were friendly and would show themselves.

'Isaac?' she called. 'Is that you?'

There was no answer.

Byron growled but did not move.

Thia stopped in her tracks.

Byron stood up for a moment. Shook himself. Then flopped down on the shady side of the tent.

Thia closed her eyes and stretched. Her back and stomach ached. The curse of being a woman, she thought. Glancing back to the bushes, she saw its eyes! Large yellow eyes, glowering at her. The yellow furry head was almost indistinguishable in the gloom of the grey-green undergrowth.

Pumas did not usually attack a man, she'd heard. But this was a big feline. Not daring to shout for Isaac for fear it might attract the cat's attention she hardly dared move. Forcing her feet to slide back slowly one after the other, she retreated.

Backing up to the tent where Byron had been lying, she was frantic. Her dog was not there. Now she could see the big cat fully. It was crawling from the bushes towards her. It stopped, crouched, preparing to spring. With her back flat against the canvas, she could go no further. Then her hand touched the long bow. She knew the quiver was beside it. Hardly daring to move, she lifted the bow and nocked an arrow. Bracing her back, she drew back the sinew string. Her arm was trembling.

The puma was ready to pounce.

'Byron,' she yelled.

With fear coursing through her veins, her arm was

157

endowed with a strength she did not know existed. She loosed the arrow. At the same moment the Newfoundland leapt at the beast placing itself between them.

Thia fell back against the canvas breaking the poles and bringing the tent down beneath her. A shot rang out and the dog and puma landed across her legs pinning her to the ground. For a moment the dog yelped and struggled. Then everything became eerily still.

'Ma'am, are you all right?' Isaac said, dropping the rifle and haring to her side.

Thia's voice was controlled. 'Get that thing off Bryon and me. We can't move under its weight.'

Isaac pushed the big cat till it rolled clear but it carried the dog with it. Its long teeth were still embedded in the Newfoundland's throat. Blood was dripping into a pool on the dirt. It was Byron's blood.

Jumping up, Thia grabbed the cat's jaw and desperately tried to prise open the massive teeth. Byron was still alive but barely. She could see he had lost much blood and he was slipping away.

With Isaac's help, she released the dog and, sitting on the ground, cradled him over her lap. She held him close to her until his paw fell from her leg and he breathed his last.

Leaving his mistress to mourn her beloved pet, Isaac dragged the still-warm cat away. His shot had only grazed its head but the arrow was embedded deep in its heart. Isaac knew it was easier to skin an animal while it was still warm. Its fur would make a beautiful rug. Once the skin was removed he could drag the carcass far from the camp and the vultures and foxes would take care of the rest.

All that remained then was to dig a grave for the Huntingley canine.

The afternoon hours dragged by slowly, but Thia waited until the others returned before laying Byron Boatswain Benedict the ninth to rest.

He was her father's dog, but he was a Huntingley dog and she loved him dearly. What would she tell Lord Beresford when she returned home? That his Newfoundland died bravely protecting her? What more could anyone wish?

When the riders returned to the camp, Bella greeted Thia wagging her tail excitedly. Thia hugged her pet before leading her to the body of her lifelong partner. His coat was still warm in the afternoon sun.

An hour later, after covering Byron with a linen shroud, Thia watched as her brother and William shovelled dirt into the grave before covering it with a cairn of stones to mark the dog's final resting place.

On a piece of wood she scratched some words she had read. They were the words Lord Byron had had engraved on a tombstone in his garden almost eighty years before:

> *Beauty without Vanity*
> *Strength without Insolence*
> *Courage without Ferocity*
> *And all the Virtues of Man without his Vices*

As the sun set over the mountains, Thia turned from the golden glow and gazed across the endless plain.

The Welshman, standing beside her, was holding the black feather in his hand.

'Now his spirit is free,' he said. 'He will run on the pampas forever.'

*

For the next few days Thia found it hard to speak to anyone. William and Algy tried hard to engage her in conversation but Davies and Ana knew that it would take time for her heart to heal. Riding along she would constantly call Bella to run beside her and would not let the Huntingley bitch out of her sight.

Having crossed a ridge, the riders were now on another plateau which stretched north, south and west. The ellusive mountains looked closer, but were still far away.

After three days' riding, Davies said they should stop. They were completely out of meat and there were herds of guanacos grazing across the plain. Each animal provided them a hundred pounds of meat and bones and if they could take two or three they would be able to ride for several days without needing to hunt. Davies and William thought the sport would be good for Thia as it would take her mind from the dead dog.

They now had only four working dogs as Martin's dogs had never been found, but with the ostrich dogs leading the chase it was not hard to run down the herd and bag three mature beasts. Jose also managed to catch an ostrich which had been lying low in the grass, sitting on a nest of eggs. Being downwind of it, the dogs had not smelt it, but Carlos's hawk eyes did not miss its head lifting from the ground.

Once the ostrich was caught, he returned and bagged almost twenty eggs. It had been a good day's hunt. There would be plenty to eat for everyone including the dogs.

The mood was positive as they rode back, Thia commenting on the thrill of the chase with no mention made of the Newfoundland. The riders were pleasantly tired and looked forward to a wholesome meal. But as they neared the camp, it was obvious something was amiss.

Algernon, who did not share his sister's delight in riding with hounds in England, had chosen to stay at the camp. He was proving to be an excellent cook and was happy in the kitchen. Isaac had stayed with him. His job was to fetch and carry and administer to the daily household chores. It was also the lad's job to collect wood, a daily necessity as they were unable to carry little more than their camping necessities with them. But it was becoming increasingly difficult to find branches or even brushwood in an area almost devoid of anything but sparse pockets of tufty grass. It was likely that the lad had to ride back to the beechwood forest to supply enough material for the fire they required for cooking.

As Isaac was efficient and industrious, it was unlikely he would have failed at his task. But the fact remained, as the riders returned they could see no smoke rising from the campsite. The sun was getting low and by this time they would have expected the fire to be burning with a pot of water boiling for coffee or the communal pot of maté, which they all now preferred.

Davies quickened his pace. It was obvious something had interrupted the day's routine.

Thia looked at William beside her as she spurred her horse, but he was oblivious that anything was wrong. Behind them, the gauchos were busy driving the pack horses loaded with the day's kill – the guanacos, skins and two ostriches, one slung on either side of Carlos's horse like feathered saddle-bags. The dogs had earned their dinner by running down the long legged birds.

Two hundred yards from the camp and it was obvious the site was empty. No one hailed them or came out to greet them as usually happened. Something was amiss.

Apart from the absence of their companions, they could see no horses and there was no sign or sound of life.

Davies's mare was fastest. He galloped toward the camp. The others followed. What a mess greeted them. Pots and pans were strewn about in the dirt. From one of the canvas packs, the bags of rice and flour had been slashed open spilling their contents across the ground.

'Where's Algy?' Williams and Thia called, almost at the same time. Quickly the pair checked in each tent, desperate to find their companion, praying they would not find him dead or injured.

'And Isaac's not here,' Thia called, turning to William. 'What has happened here?'

'I pray to God, those men have not taken them.'

Thia and William stood in the centre of the camp gazing around them not knowing what to do. Then a sudden cry struck a chill right through them.

'No!' The single word reverberated like the howl of the pampas wind. It hung on the still air as if it would never end.

'No!' the anguished cry repeated.

CHAPTER 14

The Horse

Running as fast as they could Thia and William were confronted with the scene which would wake them at night for months to come. Euan Davies was crying like a child. He was on his knees with his head buried in the thick mane of one of the Criollo horses. His bloodied hand was cupped across its nose. Its lifeless wide-set eyes glistened. A dark pool had congealed on the ground beneath the mare's mouth and the remnants of bubbled blood had formed into a pink crust around its nostrils.

'How could anyone do such a thing?' Thia cried, covering her face. 'Who would kill such fine animals?' She wanted to recognize the horse. Remember which one it was. But she couldn't. She had never ridden it, nor had any of her companions. It was just one of the spare horses used to carry the packs. A little way off was another mare. It lay in the centre of a furrowed circle, the marks carved in the ground by its hoofs as it writhed in its final agony. The silent bell hanging round its bloodstained neck would have rung out a merry accompaniment in its final minutes of life.

By now the others had joined them. Jose and Carlos regarded the scene for a moment then turned away. William took Thia in his arms. She was shaking. Seeing the silent Welshman sobbing so openly had tapped an emotion within her she didn't know she had. She wanted to comfort Euan, put her arms around him, lead him away so he could weep alone without the shame of showing his distress. Reaching out her hand she stepped towards him but Ana moved between them.

'Leave him,' the Indian woman said softly.

Thia looked questioningly into the deep pools of her Indian eyes. These were the first words Ana had spoken directly to her. How soft her voice was. It flowed smoothly despite her heavy accent.

'Tears must come. They will heal the wound,' Ana said.

Thia's tears were not only for the horse, but for the man she had known for several weeks. A man who seemed cold and withdrawn. A man who never once demonstrated the slightest hint of emotion. What was it about this pack horse which had brought him to a state of utter desolation? That question was impossible to answer.

'I pray that Algy got away before this happened,' William said.

A shiver ran through Thia's body. She had not thought about her brother's safety. 'Where is he? Where is Algy?' she cried.

'Don't worry,' William said. 'We'll find him and the boy. At least they are not here. That is some consolation.'

'But what happened? Why have these horses been shot? They have done no harm to anyone. Why weren't they taken?' Thia asked again. 'Surely good horses are worth money?'

'Not money they want, miss.' Carlos said. 'Horse not killed with gun.'

Thia looked at the gaucho demanding more.

'We call them tongue cutters. They slice tongue from horse when alive. They eat tongue while fresh and warm. They are bad men who do this. Very bad men.'

Thia grabbed for William's arm as the ground came up to meet her and the untold horrors of the Patagonian pampas engulfed her.

In the midst of the anguish and chaos, Euan Davies climbed on the back of his horse and rode off. Ana followed a few minutes later, lagging a distance behind, but making no effort to catch him.

Before he left, Davies said nothing, No one knew where he was going or when he would return. Or what they should do. Subsequently, that evening only Thia and William sat by the camp-fire but they had no appetite for the meat which Carlos cooked.

Now Davies and Ana were gone, and Algy and the boy were missing, and the perpetrators of this diabolical deed were somewhere in the vicinity. Unable to relax, the pair remained close by the fire, their rifles beside them, the dog between them, their ears alert to every sound the pampas made. Throughout the long night, the tethered horses neighed relentlessly. They had been working all day and expected to be released to graze but for this night they must stay close to the camp and could not be given their freedom.

In the firelight, Thia sipped the *yerba maté* which Jose brewed and passed to William. At midnight William took a tin of preserved fish from his saddle-bag, opened it and he and Thia shared it. She could stomach nothing more.

Next morning they took an inventory. Though the camp had been ransacked and was littered with equipment, not all the dried food or stores had been spoiled. Fortunately some of the saddle packs were spoiled. They had not been noticed as they were hidden beneath a pile of skins. And it was a great relief when Carlos returned with news that he had found the remaining spare horses. They had been grazing quietly about a mile away. Bringing back a handful of fresh mounts meant the hungry horses could be allowed their freedom.

'What do we do now?' Thia asked anxiously.

'I think we should pack up camp and go after them,' William said. 'If Algy and Isaac managed to escape from these fiends they would head to safety – back to the coast.'

'No, we cannot leave here,' said Thia. 'What if they have run away like Herr Lechter and his family and are hiding somewhere? What if they come back expecting to find us and we are not here? We cannot go. We must stay here at least until Euan returns.'

'You think Davies has gone looking for Algy?'

'Yes, don't you?'

'No. I fear in the state of mind he was in, he has gone in search of the men who did this thing to the horses.'

'Then we must go in search of Algy and the boy,' Thia said. 'They may be lost out there on the pampas. They may be on foot.'

'What if they have been taken hostage?'

'I shall not even think about that,' she said defiantly. The possibility was too diabolical to consider.

Carlos was listening. 'These men not want take English travellers to slow them down.' In his broken English he explained that evil men such as these knew nothing of the subtleties of ransom. They took what they wanted when they wanted it and life and death was balanced on the edge of a knife's blade.

After a heated debate, agreement was finally reached. They would mount up and ride out leaving no one behind at the camp. But they would leave a message for Algernon in case he returned. They agree to search for three days returning to the camp each night. If, at the end of that time, they had not located the pair and Davies had not returned, they would pack up their camp and return to Sandy Point in the vain hope that they would find them there safe and well.

The expedition was now reduced to four riders, Thia and William, Jose and Carlos. Taking Jose's advice they decided to head back towards the beechwood ridge – where Thia had killed the puma. At least that area would be familiar to the English aristocrat and his servant and by going there they would be travelling in the opposite direction to that which they presumed the prison escapees were going.

They had been riding for two hours when Carlos reined in his horse. He had the best eyes for spotting guanaco or ostriches and he had seen something on the horizon.

Alarmed and excited at the same time, Thia gazed ahead but could see nothing but a small cloud of dust, little more than a ball of fluff in the distance. They stopped and waited.

From the cloud emerged four riders and several horses and they were galloping towards them. Were they about to be attacked? Thia reached for her rifle but Jose lifted his arm and pointed.

'Welsh Euan, he come back. With him two lost English men and squaw.'

Thia and William were ecstatic. They craned their necks

and squinted in an effort to identify the riders. Once they were sure all was well, Thia and William spurred their horses and rode out to meet their companions. It was a joyful reunion. How happy Thia was to see her brother back safely, and Isaac, and also Euan and Ana. She still wondered why the Indian woman followed the Welshman everywhere but was still reticent to ask what relationship existed between them.

That evening there was non-stop chatter between Thia, her brother and William. The others sitting nearby watched but said little. Everyone ate well and relaxed, and no mention was made of the dead horses or the men who had killed them.

Bella rolled on her back and then sank down next to Thia who combed her fingers through her dog's coat. It was long and coarse but the undercoat was thick and soft as a carpet of gossamer. Such a canine would never suffer the cold, not even on the ice fields of the Andes Mountains.

'Algy,' she said, turning to her brother. 'I am so proud of you. You were so clever to escape from those men.'

'But our camp was destroyed and we lost almost everything,' he said.

'Not all was lost and who cares anyway,' William said. 'You are safe and that is the main thing.'

Algernon smiled. 'I regard my actions rather like the way I play chess. I am always on the run and end up forfeiting the board to my opponent. Is that not so, William?'

'That is not quite how I would describe what happened here, Algy, but by forfeiting the camp you certainly saved yourself and won the game in my eyes.'

Algernon laughed. He was as relaxed as if he were sitting in the drawing-room at Huntingley. 'Then I must give you lessons in my strategy, William. And I must tell you all about the Indian camp. It would make a fine scene for a theatre production. Actually, if truth be told, Isaac and I had little time to be alarmed. It all happened so quickly. The Indians who brought the warning were very polite though it was a tolerably difficult job to understand their broken English.' He laughed again. 'I think also they would benefit from your schooling in table manners. During the course of the evening meal I was hard pressed to keep a straight face. But at no time was I afraid of them.'

'And what about you, Isaac? Did they treat you well?'

'Never better, ma'am. I watched a lady making a pair of boots from the skins off a guanaco's legs. She made the hock into the heel and sewed them up with a needle made of bone. I will do that with a goat or boar skin one day.'

'Not quite as soft as guanaco, I think,' William said.

Isaac had to agree.

The conversation continued for several hours and, though they were all tired, they were loath to part from each other's company. Sitting together, sharing another brew, they watched the sun setting slowly over the mountains; the heavens changing colours – mauve, pink, lilac, blue, indigo, grey – a moving canopy of colour painting the sky.

'How stark and beautiful this place is,' William said. 'If I had a glass of wine, I would propose a toast. But I shall propose it anyway. To Patagonia – a place we will never forget.'

Thia and her brother clinked their imaginary glasses as the sun finally slid behind the mountain peaks and the night folded down like a concertina curtain. Layer upon layer, pink on mauve, purple on blue, grey on navy. Dropping slowly. Pressing every ounce of pigment into the final few inches of sky in a fiery display of burnt orange. Polished mahogany. Burnished gold. The rich colour reflected in the skin of the Tehuelche Indians.

CHAPTER 15

Kattn

'You ride with the hunt at home, I presume?' the Welshman said.

'Of course. At least once a month.'

'Do you find that agreeable?'

'It is good sport, but I see from your expression you do not approve.'

'No, I do not.'

'But you shoot the guanaco and ostrich, birds and fowl.'

'But not the way you do. I do not kill them for pleasure as you English do; three dozen brave men and fifty hounds glee-fully chasing a defenceless fox and seeing it ripped to pieces. I kill only for food as other carnivorous animals do and I ask no man to do my killing. I think you forget you expect others to kill for you. The fowl on your dinner table had been bagged by your gamekeeper. The suckling pig wrenched by the crofter from the sow's teat. The cattle taken from the meadow and slaughtered by the butcher. I do it all myself but only when it is necessary.'

Thia didn't answer. She had killed the puma in self-defence and she had chased the ostrich and guanaco and shot a few and they had cooked and shared the meat amongst them. But what he was saying about killing for sport rang true. How would she feel when she was back amongst the likes of Amanda Trenby? How could she get excited following a fox? Nothing would be the same again.

They stopped for a while and dismounted. Ahead the land dropped into a depression. The water had mostly drained from it leaving a lake of salt. It had a strange purple colouration and wading on its banks was a huge flock of pink flamingos.

Thia shook her head in amazement. 'There is something about this place which is indescribable. It is so barren yet it holds such peace and magnificent solitude. It is like being in a ruined abbey – it has an ambiance which is close to Godliness. I cannot explain it.'

'That is something that I have often thought about. But, like you, I cannot explain that feeling to anyone who has never visited this place. Patagonia has a voice and once you leave it, it calls you back. It is like good wine, it intoxicates without making you drunk as you savour the smell of its delicate flavour. If I could bottle it, I could make a fortune,' he said, smiling.

It was the first time she had seen him looking so relaxed. And though his moustache hid the corner of his lips the smile radiated from his eyes.

They watched the flock of flamingos wading, their plumage changing from rose to white and back to pink as the wind ruffled their feathers.

'Tell me about your hurt, Euan. Tell me about the dead horses and the men who mutilated them.'

The Welshman straightened defensively.

'I am sorry, I should not ask.'

Not taking his eyes from the purple water, he breathed deeply. Paused. Then spoke. 'Those men are evil.'

Thia's voice was soft. 'Are they the reason for you being here?'

'Yes, they are the reason I came back to Patagonia. I intend to kill them.'

Sitting beside him, hardly daring to move in case she interrupted his thoughts, she waited for a while. 'Can you tell me why?'

'I spoke to you about the riot in 1877 when the prisoners escaped from the garrison and rioted, killing and mutilating the guards and many of the townsfolk.'

'I remember.'

'It is now eight years since that happened but for me it is as fresh in my mind as if it had happened yesterday.'

'Do not tell me if it pains you.'

'It is time to tell.'

'I had bought land on Tierra del Fuego. I had sheep and the natives continued to steal them until one day I visited their camp and gave them some horses as a gift. In time I got to know them well and they trusted me.'

'Your wife was an Indian.'

'Yes, she was a full blood Tehuelche from the mainland. I called her Kattn because the word reminded me of a kitten. It means *soft* in her language.' He sighed again. 'No man has ever so devoted a wife as a man married to one of the natives. Kattn followed me everywhere and did everything she could to please me. We were together for two years. Two wonderful years I will never forget.'

'Were you on the island during the riot?'

'No, we had paddled across to Sandy Point in a canoe. I wanted to order some more sheep for my farm. We did not stay in the town. As you can see it is a God-forsaken place and was more so then. Instead we hired horses and rode ten miles from town and made our camp there.

'During the evening, even from that distance we could hear the canon being fired from the garrison and we saw smoke. We could see that the town was burning. I wanted to ride back to help but Kattn wouldn't let me go alone. She said she would come with me. Not wanting anything to happen to her I agreed to stay. I told her we would both go in the morning.

'That night we slept only fitfully. We could hear gunfire not very far away. I remember it was a cold night but beneath our furs the heat of our combined bodies kept us wonderfully warm.'

Thia smiled. She was pleased to hear him talk. It was unusual for even a woman to talk to her of such matters. But talk of his body did not shock her. She had never experienced someone else's warmth close to her – not even her mother's.

A gust of wind whistled across the lake disturbing the birds which sprang up flapping their wings.

'I remember getting up twice through the night to settle the horses. We had tethered them to the bushes so we would not have to go searching for them in the morning.

'The third time I awoke, I sensed something was wrong. The fire was almost out and the pale moon was flickering from behind the rolling clouds. It was an ominous night and the horses were agitated. At first I thought it was a puma prowling nearby. Then I heard the clink of metal spurs.

'I ran back to the tent and grabbed my knife which was beside my saddle. There was no time to load the rifle. As I

174

came from the tent, four men rushed at me out of the darkness. They yelled and screamed like drunken banshees waking my wife. I tried my best to stave them off and yelled for her to grab a horse and run. Kattn could ride like the wind and could have got away from them if she had wanted. But she wouldn't leave.' He shook his head. 'It was not the kind of fight you would ever wish to witness. I sliced one in the leg and he fell away and I gouged the eye from another. But I saw nothing after that save the barrel of a rifle pointed at my head. I remember trying to twist away to avoid the bullet, but I wasn't quick enough. That was the last I remember until I awoke.'

Thia waited.

'It was the strangest awakening. Like being in a dream where one cannot run. Not only could I not run but I could hardly breathe and could barely move an inch from the hunched position I was in. There were voices, echoing voices and raucous laughter but my brain would not wake to it. The easiest option was to allow sleep to overcome me and let the dream take its course. But of course it was not a dream. The taste of blood was real. The smell of the freshly killed guanaco hide was real. The sound of my wife's cries was only too real also.'

She watched the pain contort his face.

'It had been dark, but now it was light. The four men had gone and it was raining.' He laughed weakly. 'Imagine that happening in a place where it rains infrequently. It was cold sleety rain. I could feel it running down my face. It woke me up and it was the only thing which saved me.'

They watched in silence as the flock of flamingos took to the air and the rose-pink cloud headed north.

'Do you want to continue,' Thia asked.

175

'I do not think you would want to hear any more.'

'I would like to be able to understand.'

'Let us walk a while.'

Thia picked up her hat, and the scarf she used to secure it to her head. 'What happened to Kattn, your wife?'

'They raped her and when they had done with her they pegged her naked body on the cold earth in the fashion they did with Martin. They used thongs of freshly skinned leather to tie her arms and legs so that when the sun rose, if she had survived the night's chill and the mountain lions and biting insects, the leather would dry and when it shrank it would slowly wrench her arms from her body. Hopefully, the thong they tied around her neck would strangle her before that occurred.'

'Were you awake when this was happening?'

'No. The bullet had glanced across my temple taking off the tip of my ear.' Lifting back his hair, he revealed a notch in his ear. 'I do not know how long I slept as when I awoke from my stupor, the sun had risen, and apart from the birds, everything was silent.'

'You said you couldn't move. Were you paralysed?

'It felt like it. No, these men had learned their tortures in the north. They took the fresh skins which I had hung to dry only a couple of hours earlier. They wrapped me in the skin, trussed me like a turkey in a sack, and secured it around my neck. Only my head stuck out. The thong around my neck had been twisted with a stake through it. As the thong dried I would be slowly throttled and if not I would be crushed within the skin as it dried and shrank. The effect is like a vice.'

'Yet you managed to escape.'

'Only with God-given luck, because my brain was slow to function.'

'Did the rain save you?'

'Indeed. The skin was still wet with its natural juices and the rain made it wetter. So long as a skin does not dry, it will not shrink.'

'But if it was tied at the neck, how did you get out of it?'

'At first I tried to chew at the leather, but every time I moved my head the thong bit tighter around my throat. Then I remembered the blade which I carry slipped in the seam of my trouser leg. Look here,' he said, taking her hand and running her fingers down the stitching on the outer part of his calf. 'I still carry it today. You would not know I had anything concealed there, would you?'

Thia nodded as she watched him slide the stiletto from its narrow stitched leather sheath.

'I have carried this since I was a young man and it has saved my life more than once.'

'You managed to retrieve it and cut your way out of the skin?'

He nodded gazing into the distance. 'The mountains see many things, yet they say nothing. They tell no lies but they reveal no truths either. Do they laugh at us mere mortals or cry for us? Sometimes I wonder.'

'Was your wife still alive?'

'Barely. I untied her and gently dusted the dirt from her face. Then I carried her limp body to our shelter and laid her on guanaco skins and took off my clothes and lay beside her. She was so cold she was beyond shivering. I did not want to fall asleep and tried hard to stay awake but my strength was exhausted and my mind succumbed easily. When I woke, I found she had breathed her last. Her head was resting on my shoulder. The dried blood from her mouth was on my cheek.'

Thia found it hard to speak. 'You said farewell to her there.'

'I should have buried her there, seated in a grave, facing west. That is the custom. But I had no spade and I could not dig into the hard ground with my hands. Instead I burned her body on a funeral pyre. The only spirits who were present besides me were the condors who circled the sky above. The four men were long gone as were my horses, my water, my rifles and my rations.'

'Did you keep anything to remind you of your wife?'

He looked at her resentfully.

'I am sorry. I should not have asked such a personal question.'

'I should not have done. When an Indian dies the custom is to burn everything they have. If a man dies and he has twenty horses, the family will slaughter all the animals. Nothing is passed on as in England. A son must make his own fortune.' As he spoke he took a soft vellum pouch from his coat pocket. In it was a switch of jet-black hair. It had been plaited.

'May I?' asked Thia, not knowing whether he would want her to touch it.

He was cautious before allowing her hand to rest on it.

'You took it as a keepsake.'

'Yes. I should have burned it but I wanted to keep something.'

'To remember her by?'

'No,' he said, turning it to reveal the strip of skin which prevented the hair from separating. 'They scalped her then they cut out her tongue.'

Thia shuddered. 'Are these the same men who are loose on the pampas now?'

'Yes.'

'But how did you find out.'

'Two months ago in Liverpool, I received word that they

had escaped from the prison in Buenos Ayres. I did not know which way they were heading. They could have gone north to Brazil or Mexico or south to Patagonia. I guessed they would head south and my assumption was correct.'

'What do you know of them?'

'They are all Chilotes. They come from the Island of Chiloe across the other side of the Andes. They were some of the ringleaders in the Sandy Point massacre. They are evil men and I will never forget their faces.'

'And what will you do now?'

'I came here to find them and when I find them I will kill them.'

That night Algernon invited Davies to join them. There were things they had to discuss.

The Welshman agreed and asked if Ana could be included.

After eating and sharing the maté, Thia spoke. 'Algy, William and I are all agreed; if you will allow us to ride with you, we will help you to find these men, but we believe they should be brought back to face a proper trial.'

'The legal system in this country is almost non existent. Here people take justice into their own hands and criminals do not wait around to be caught.'

'But these men came back to Sandy Point. Why was that?'

'They are rotten through and through and have no conscience. They were locked away in prison for heinous acts before the riots and they have not changed. When they escaped from the garrison with the rest of the prisoners they behaved like wild animals, raping and killing and it was only when they were starving on the pampas that they were caught and taken to Buenos Ayres. Everyone expected the ringleaders to be hanged, but the Chilean and Argentinean authorities could not agree what to do with them so they were put in prison there. Hopefully to be left to die. I thought that was the last I would hear of them, but now four of them are back. Perhaps they have heard of the gold which is being sifted from the black sand at Cape Virgenes or the mines on Tierra del Fuego.'

'You think they would work?'

'Not them. They look for easy pickings. To steal from the men who work hard for their bag of gold dust.'

'Will they be looking for you,' Algernon asked.

'What interest am I to them? None. Just another of their victims. I doubt they would remember my face or my wife who they killed for nothing more than their own sadistic amusement. But I will never forget them and if the opportunity arises, I will kill them with my bare hands, I promise.'

'You think they are planning to cross the mountains?'

'Yes, I do.'

'Do they know you are following them?'

'No. Not yet.'

'But they came to our camp. Killed the horses.'

'To the camp of a group of rich Englishmen. You are no threat to them. You are just foolish travellers. But, be mindful, they will not think twice of killing you all should your paths cross.'

'What if they cannot cross the Andes and decide to retrace their steps, where would they go?'

'Across the pampas to Chubut, the Welsh settlement. Or east to the port of Saint Julian or Port Desire where they could board a ship to take them to Monte Video. Once there they will be safe. They will disappear into the populace for as long as it suits them.'

'Whichever way you go, you should not go alone.'

'I will not be alone, Ana will ride with me.'

'Is Ana your new wife?' Thia asked politely.

'No. But as she has no brothers, she has promised her father she will not return to her people until the men responsible for Kattn's death are dead.'

'Which way will you go?'

'West to the Cordillera. That is the way those men are heading. For your own safety, you must all return to Sandy Point. Jose and Carlos will ride with you and make sure you arrive there safely. Once you reach the estancia Señor Garcia will welcome you into his home until the next ship arrives to take you to Buenos Ayres.'

It was with heavy hearts and mixed feeling that they breakfasted the following morning. Little was said as they packed their provisions, distributing a proportion to Davies and Ana but the rest being taken by the Huntingley party and their two guides. Davies only accepted one spare horse though the frugal amount he carried would have packed on the back of his own mount. Thia was alarmed at how light he was travelling, but he assured her he had all he required; he could kill enough food to feed the pair of them. Carlos gave him his two dogs in exchange for some skins. Davies was happy with the trade as he did not want to carry the excess items into the mountains. He had sufficient furs and they both had their *capas* for warmth and bedding. The dogs would certainly be useful.

Sitting astride his mount, Thia looked up at the Welshman. He had been carrying much more than a physical burden with him. Having shared his story, she hoped it had lightened the weight of that terrible incident he had experienced. She knew the memory of it would never leave him, but now he seemed more relaxed and even smiled occasionally. She doubted he would change his resolve to kill the four men but his passion for revenge was not as powerful as it had previously been.

With his *capa* beneath him on the saddle, his *bolas* and *lazo* on the pommel, he tipped his hat to the English expedition and rode away. Ana followed, her Criollo horse staying a few paces behind.

'Her heart is as deep and silent as the pampas,' Thia said. 'It is as though she is in tune with the vast countryside around her. A kind of innate animism which native people possess which we civilized people seem to have lost.'

William had no answer. There was certainly something about this native Indian woman which he could not explain. Without meaning or intention, she attracted him like a pin to a magnet, yet she hardly ever spoke, showed little expression, even conserved her gestures to essential movements. She was as tall as a longbow and moved like a willow in the breeze. Was as strong as any man he knew and slightly taller than he. She was not beautiful by English standards with her plucked eyebrows and painted skin, but she had the elongated face and forehead of the high priestesses he had seen engraved on the walls of the ancient temples in Cairo. Now he wished he had drawn her portrait as he could never replicate it accurately. Yet her face was engrained in his mind and he knew he would never forget it.

He raised his arm and waved. 'God Speed!' he shouted, but the pair was already half a mile away, heading west. He doubted they would hear his voice.

'Do you think we will ever see them again, sir?' Isaac asked.

'I pray so,' William said.

Thia sighed wearily. 'I hope he never finds the men he is chasing for I fear what the outcome will be.'

No one was prepared to answer.

CHAPTER 16

Fending for themselves

There was an air of disappointment as they rode from the camp. They had covered many miles on their journey but would never climb to the snow-line or stand in the shadow of the ragged peaks. But none of them was sorry to be leaving the campsite where the attack on the horses had taken place.

A chill ran though Thia as she recounted the things they had seen; of the blood and anguish and pain they caused everyone, especially the Welshman. It seemed that it all happened long ago yet it was only yesterday and by now the men responsible could be fifty miles away. She wondered why they had only taken four horses but left the rest. As Euan said, the escapees saw no danger in a group of English travellers trying to mimic the life of a gaucho.

Heading back, Carlos chose to take a different route from the one they had come on. He explained in broken English that Welsh Euan had suggested they cross the river at a different point where there was a natural ford. The wild horses would have decimated the winding track which they had traversed down the side of the ravine to such an extent that it would have been foolish to climb it. After William's fall and near drowning they all accepted the change of route willingly. That was a concern they had all carried but no one had mentioned it.

Instead of heading east, they were travelling north in the shadow of a ridge covered in a dense growth of beechwood. With no tracks through it they had to travel to the end of the plateau. In the cool of the morning it was a pleasant ride. Carlos and Jose rode ahead with the three Huntingley companions. Isaac tagged along behind, his horse flanked by Bella and Jose's two dogs who all tolerated each other reasonably well.

At times they cantered or broke into a swinging gallop but with the steamer due in at Sandy Point later that week and no hope of meeting it, they knew they did not have to hurry in order to be there for the next one. The hunting they had done the previous day had provided them with two guanaco carcasses and three young rheas. They also carried a mounting supply of ostrich eggs which fortunately would keep for as long as necessary. Now there were only six of them in the group to feed, plus three dogs. They had exhausted the onions and had very little rice after much had been spilled or stolen, but they still had a bag of biscuits and plenty of leaf for the maté.

As they rounded the ridge, they could see the pampas again looming as broad as an endless sea. It was barren and treeless and appeared to have no contours, though they knew that one plateau dropped to another, and then another, as the land slowly descended to the east coast. Ahead was the river valley snaking away to the south and east, like a single pencil line drawn on a map. Its immense width and depth was

185

deceptive but they had to cross it.

Following its course for some time, they were amazed at the strips of green bordering the broad river-bed. Here its flow was slower than the rushing torrent they remembered. But it was much wider – twice the width of the Thames at Westminster Bridge. Hopefully it was not as deep. Carlos and Jose suggested that they set up camp at the bottom of the valley and allowed the horses freedom to graze overnight. There would be enough driftwood around for a fire and the opportunity to bathe for the first time in several days appealed to them all.

They rode for half an hour, before Carlos indicated the path down. This was also a thoroughfare used by the wild horses, but it was a gradual decline and the other side of the ravine appeared quite gentle also.

Again they did not reach the bottom without some slight mishap. Algernon's horse's hoof cracked on the sharp rocks and, as it stumbled, he was almost unseated. Fortunately he was able to dismount and continue on foot to the river below. Now they only had five spare horses carrying the camping equipment. It was possible they would have to leave some non essentials behind.

After dinner, Jose, Carlos and Isaac rode out of the valley, back to the edge of the beechwood forest. They wanted to collect wood for the evening's fire and make up several additional bundles; sufficient to last them for the next two nights. As they traversed the pampas, the Indian women collected every last twig that was blown there leaving nothing that was combustible. But a supply of firewood for cooking and warmth was essential and after her confrontation with the puma, Thia was always pleased to see a bright fire blazing when she lay down under her furs at night.

It was dark in the canyon when they returned with an enormous quantity of branches which were stacked high on the back of the two pack horses. Yet the news they brought was disturbing.

With his remarkable vision, Carlos, *The Titan*, had spotted smoke. It was on the same side of the river but far away to the north-west. His instinct told him it was not Indians.

'Could it be the four men Mr Davies is searching for?'

Carlos nodded, as he drew on his pipe. '*Mañana*, I find out. No good Welsh Euan heading to Cordillera if men going in opposite direction.'

If it were true, Davies was heading away on a wild goose chase.

'Then he will kill no one,' Thia said, relieved that he would not have their blood on his hands.

'But those men must be stopped or they will go on reeking havoc on anyone or anything in their path. If anyone can stop them it is Euan,' William said.

William was right, though the prospect of becoming embroiled in another meeting with the Chilotes was not what they wanted.

'Tomorrow, you go look,' Thia said, to the gaucho. 'But be careful they do not see you. Find out if it is those men.'

Carlos merely nodded. Jose continued sharpening his knife without even looking up.

To the group of travellers, it appeared that gaucho blood diluted the fear and apprehension which flowed so readily through English veins.

The Titan left early insisting on riding alone. One horse would throw up less dust and he could travel fast. He knew the distance which most men's eyes could see ahead of them, and knew his exceptional vision allowed him to view his quarry well before it saw him.

Jose and Isaac offered to take turns as lookouts on the top of the ravine while below Thia and her companions loaded their rifles and revolvers as a precaution against a surprise attack. The horses that had grazed were tethered to stakes set in the ground. They needed them close by and could not afford to lose them at this stage.

As the morning drew on, apprehension hung like a damp blanket over the encampment. Fearing the worst, no one spoke for if Carlos had been seen by the four men they might have chased him and he could have already suffered the same fate meted out to poor Martin.

But Jose seemed unconcerned. 'Carlos good gaucho,' he said. 'He will return.' Within minutes Isaac appeared on the track. 'He's coming,' he shouted excitedly. Then he turned and rode back up to meet the returning horseman.

Everyone was pleased to see him and to get news.

'Is it them?' Thia asked.

'Yes,' he said, sliding from his horse.

'Can you be sure?'

'I saw four men go away from camp where I saw the smoke. They did not see me. They rode slowly. Then I went to their camp. They left things they had stolen. Empty tins – fish, milk. Indians do not eat from tins and if they find, they make into something useful. Not leave behind. It is the same men.'

'Jose, you must ride. Go find Welsh Euan and bring him back here,' Thia said.

Algernon looked doubtful. 'But it could take three days to catch up with him and three days to return. By then these villains will be long gone and we will never find them.'

'Men heading for Saint Julian,' Carlos added. 'They use Indian track. Everyone on pampas knows Indian track.'

'Then even if it takes a week we will be able to follow them, is that right, Carlos?'

The gaucho nodded.

With only strips of dried roasted meat and some dry biscuits in his saddle-bag and his skins for shelter, Jose was despatched to find the Welshman and Ana. Isaac volunteered to ride with him and, though the young groom had proved to be an excellent horseman, the gaucho declined. He could ride faster on his own.

If he failed to find the pair, he promised to return within seven days. During that time the group would have to stay at the same camp in the valley. At least it provided shelter from the wind, plenty of fresh water, and ample grazing for the horses. But there were two dangers. If there was a summer downpour on the mountains, a sudden torrent of water could wash down the ravine carrying their camp away with it. A stampede of several hundred wild horses thundering along the valley could have an equally devastating effect. But there were other things to worry about as well. Jose's horse could fall or run off at night. Then there was the possibility the escapees would double back and surprise them. The only consolation they could find was that while they waited they could replenish their supplies of firewood and meat, bathe and wash their clothes. But they would have to keep constant watch both day and night and waiting would not be easy.

Only two days had passed when Isaac came galloping frantically down the side of the ravine. A cloud of dust was being kicked up in the distance. A group of riders was approaching. They were riding hard and directly towards the canyon. It was time to put in place the plan they had agreed on under such circumstances. They must stay low in the camp by the river and hope that had not been seen. If they were attacked they would defend themselves as best they could.

William squeezed Thia's hand reassuringly. She picked up her revolver. They could hear stones bouncing down the side of the ravine and the clattering of horses' hoofs. Bella barked and the two ostrich dogs ran out towards the noise.

With her heart thumping in her throat, Thia hardly dare take a breath, then she heard Euan's voice.

'*Hola*! Don't fire!'

'We rode for half a day searching for their tracks but could not find any. When we reached the next river, it was obvious they had not attempted a crossing. The river was flowing too strongly and if they had tried to swim across they would have been washed back to the same side. Knowing there were several rivers ahead and the spring thaw had come late, they probably decided that their chances of fording them and then crossing the mountains was nigh impossible.'

'Did you find their tracks?'

'Only after doubling back and swimming the horses across at the ford. Their tracks were easy to follow and I quickly realized that they were heading east. My concern was that they might have crossed your path and discovered you here. Fortunately Carlos spotted me only a day's ride from here. Thank God he has the eyes of a hawk.'

Delighted to see him back, Thia hugged him. His presence gave her the confidence she realized she sometimes lacked.

'So,' he said, 'we know they are heading east. They will attempt to make Port Saint Julian or Santa Cruz.'

'Then this time you must allow us to ride with you,' Thia

said. 'We cannot return to Sandy Point until these men are brought to justice. Together we number eight, plus the dogs. William is an excellent shot and we are all good riders. We will not slow you. And if the journey takes us all the way to the coast, we will take a ship from there to the Rio de la Plata and connect with the steamship in Monte Video.'

'But your brother Algernon, is he in agreement?'

Thia looked maternally at her brother who was drawing water from the river.

'Algy is a kind and good-hearted man who, out of choice, would not hurt a fly. But we have spoken of this in the last two days and his abhorrence at the things these men have done has determined him to support whatever we feel is necessary. Algy may appear soft, but he is no coward and during the course of this *holiday* he has revealed an inner strength and determination I had never seen before. Trust me he will not let you down.'

'Then so be it. We will proceed together but from now on you must promise never to go anywhere alone. We must stay together as a group. Besides being evil, these men are cunning and, believing they are invulnerable, have no fear of anyone or anything. Their tricks are dirty and we may have to play them at their own game. It will not be played according to the rules attributed to the Marquis of Queensbury.

'In the meantime, I suggest you learn to use the *bolas*. I will make some for you. And with your skill with the bow, it may be worth carrying such a silent weapon. From here we must travel swiftly and stealthily and you must learn to use the guile and imagination of a native.'

CHAPTER 17

The Peat Bog

For two days they travelled at a slow pace following the tracks left by the four Chilotes. They were heading east, descending from one plateau to another by way of another broad ravine. Ahead the pampas was flat, a monotonous prairie which stretched as far as the eye could see. With no trees or bush to provide any cover, Davies was not anxious to hurry. He did not want to confront his quarry on the open steppes. Staying at a respectable distance allowed them to burn a fire at night without fear of the smoke being seen. It also allowed them to see the camp-fires lit by the men they were stalking.

'We won't lose them,' Davies said. 'They are leaving good tracks.'

'Let us hope the pampas wind is not on their side,' Thia said.

With time to waste, Jose, Carlos and the dogs split from the group. A flock of six young rheas had attracted the dogs' attention and they needed no prompting to chase the birds.

With heads poking forward almost parallel to the ground and wings outstretched, the birds fairly flew. As the dogs bounded closer they suddenly changed direction and doubled back but the dogs, unable to pull up with such speed, rolled over in the dirt. Taking the *bolas* which was wrapped around his upper body, Jose swung them in a circle. The round stones hummed as they rotated faster and faster on the ends of the leather thongs. Aiming for one of the rheas, he let the *bolas* fly. The thongs circled around the bird's neck and swung down entangling its legs. Once on the ground, the ostrich's fate was sealed. Jose jumped down and broke its neck. Within a matter of minutes the dogs were rewarded with a feed of offal and the bird was slung across Jose's saddle. Half a mile away Carlos had similar success. There would be rib of roast ostrich for dinner that evening.

When they joined the English party, Davies pointed to some black specks in the sky. At first Thia could not see them. but as they rode on, they became clearer. Wheeling high on the thermals of hot air was a group of six black birds. They seemed not to be moving and looked so small but Thia remembered what Isaac had told her; a twelve foot wingspan and a body which stood two feet high on the ground. Condors.

Davies glanced at the gauchos. Could be a dead guanaco or a nest of ostrich eggs deliberately broken up by the male bird after being disturbed.

They rode on for several miles, the pampas plateau broken by a long depression – the dry bed of an ancient river which had long since changed its track. In the distance was a large lake fed by rain and spring melt water. The green forest and bushes which surrounded it was a welcome sight to the travellers' eyes after the morose greyness of the monotonous plains they had been riding over. But before they dropped down into the valley Davies halted, pointing towards the verdant pockets of green. They looked inviting and the horses could already smell the grass. They reined in and followed Davies as he started his descent down the hillside.

'Stay behind me,' he shouted.

Being a well worn formation, the gradient was not steep, but they followed his instructions not knowing what was ahead and the reason for his caution.

When he reached bottom he called a halt and dismounted.

'Stay there,' he said, beckoning Jose and Carlos to join him.

Fifty yards ahead was a dead fireplace and close by a shelter of twined branches in the form of a primitive tent.

The three horsemen wandered around the campsite from all directions, stepping carefully, scanning the ground, quickly forming a picture of who had been there and what had happened.

Thia and the others dismounted but remained where they had been left until Davies came back and joined them.

'A small group of Indians were here. They left very early this morning.'

'Is that a concern?'

'They had visitors.'

'Unwelcome guests?'

'I fear so. There is blood on the ground. If it were an animal's blood there would be bits of fur scattered around. There is none. At least one person was injured.'

'Then it is likely the men we are after were responsible.'

Davies nodded. 'They were either extremely hungry or extremely foolish – probably both – to attack this camp. There would have been more than half-a-dozen Indians in this camp and their women.'

'Do you think they got what they were looking for?'

'It is impossible to say. There was a great disturbance around where the horses were grazing.'

'Perhaps it was fresh horses they were after.'

'It is hard to know as there are many tracks leading away but I think the Indians were ready for them and chased them off.'

'Then they may have done the job you have come here to do,' Thia said.

'There is no evidence of that. All I know is that a group of riders galloped off towards the lake. Perhaps we will find something there.'

The group remounted, eager to ride ahead, but the Welshman insisted they stay behind him. Ahead the gentle contours of the valley's sides were lifeless carrying only the stubble of an ancient forest, but at the bottom, the valley burst into life. Trees, bushes and shrubs flourished circling an huge arena of open ground. It was covered with a carpet of yellow green moss and from a distance was a welcome oasis. The riders stayed close behind Davies as he rode directly towards it.

Jose slowed, examined the ground and suddenly galloped up the hillside. 'Three went this way,' he called, when he reached the top.

'Many horses stop here. One horse go across here,' Carlos said, pointing.

Thia and her companions looked in the direction he was indicating.

This area was not the attractive oasis they had envisaged, but a peat bog made from layers of humus and dead trees accumulated hundreds of years ago.

'Don't walk on the moss,' he said, looking down at the marks imprinted on the spongy edges – the evidence of a single horse racing across at a full gallop.

Taking each step as gingerly as a crane walking on waterlily leaves, the Newfoundland bitch padded out on to the surface, its broad webbed feet splayed like cushions so as not to sink. How different its feet were to the sharp hoofs of a guanaco or horse which would immediately pierce through the soft mesh of tangled mosses.

Anxiously, Thia called her dog to heel.

Bella returned wagging her tail as a vulture swept past. The whoosh of its wings pulsed like the sound of a windmill's weather vane beating on the wind.

'Over there,' Davies shouted, pointing to a venue of vultures only twenty yards away. One of the ugly birds was perched on a carved butt of wood – the hilt of a rifle. Beside it another bird danced up and down on the bare bone of a horse's leg. Beside it, the raised mound of white ribs delineated the equine's belly. The skin and muscle had been ripped open. The sinew and entrails plucked out. Close by the horse's mane decorated the mossy surface. It was draped like dried seaweed deposited on a deserted beach.

'My God, what happened?'

'I believe one of the riders made a bad decision. He thought this was the quickest way out of the valley and foolishly tried to ride across the peat. Be careful! It is like quicksand,' Davies said. 'At the edges it is still hard and he could have galloped across for a few yards. But only his momentum would have carried him forward. Where the bog softens his horse would have attempted to kick its way forward but it would have only succeeded in digging itself deeper in the mire. Eventually the bog would have swallowed it.'

'And what of the rider, could he have dragged himself out?'

196

'Not if he tried to swim; he too would have dug himself in deeper. See, he is still there. Near the rifle butt you can see a crown of white poking up from the blackness. The birds have cleaned the flesh from his skull already. Engulfed in the peat, the rest of his body will be preserved for centuries.'

Thia shuddered. 'Could the Indians have pulled him out?'

'They know these sorts of swamps and would not venture out on it at this time of the year.'

'Then they would have left the man to drown?'

'They could have put a bullet through his head, but that would have been too kind.'

'What a way to die!' William said.

Davies did not answer. He retuned to his horse. 'Now we have only three men to find. The odds are improving.'

Davies looked at the still circling condors as the evening sky turned through its rainbow of colours, red, orange, yellow, blue, indigo, violet. Only moss-green was missing.

'I have never seen such skies in England.'

'Nor I,' he said. 'It has been said that this land was the last place on earth which God created. That he used all the pieces He had left over, the deserts, plateaux, mountains, rivers, lakes and glaciers. Not wanting to waste anything He threw them all together and created the tail end of the earth.'

'You love this place, don't you?'

Euan nodded.

'Will you stay here or go back to England when this business is concluded?'

'It is a lonely place. The loneliest place on earth. It is also cold. So cold for such a long time I sometimes wonder how I have survived it. But Kattn was my warmth. Like all the Tehuelche Indians she did not seem to feel it. They can go

197

naked in the coldest weather and do not appear to suffer from it. But because my English skin is thin, I come here only in the summertime.'

'Then who tends your farm when you are away.'

'I have a manager.'

'So will you go back to England when we do?'

'I do not know. Perhaps I will build a house in Sandy Point. The town is growing fast.'

'Will you return to the Land of Fire?'

'Not to live alone.'

'Then you will take another wife?'

He smiled. 'An Indian? No, I could never do that.'

As they spoke the smoke from the camp-fire swirled up to the darkening sky.

At the other side of the campsite William's blond hair glowed golden in the sunset and his tanned skin appeared almost as rich as that of the Indian woman sitting beside him. They did not speak but there was no evidence of embarrassment. William was comfortable with Ana's silence. He always sat beside her when they ate and offered her biscuits and water to which she never graced him with a please or thank you.

He wore the brightly coloured fillet she had woven for him around his forehead and with the poncho he had purchased from the Indians, his dress resembled that of a native. In the daylight however, his blond curly hair could never disguise his Anglo Saxon blood.

CHAPTER 18

The Man on the Horse

Across the bare plain, a plume of dust was just visible in the far distance. Thia could not distinguish what was causing it but after discounting it being the three Chilotes, she considered it was a pack of wild horses or a herd of guanacos. The South American ostriches usually only appeared individually or in small numbers and did not run in large troops.

When Carlos burst into a gallop they all did likewise. With his remarkable vision, they all trusted his decisions.

After ten minutes' hard riding they were close enough to identify a single rider chasing a group of guanacos. They all recognized the brightly coloured poncho he was wearing – it was Martin's.

Davies signalled for them all to slow. He wanted to ensure that the man was alone and that the other two men were not hunting in the same area. Had the three men split up to go hunting? Or had they argued and decided to travel separately? That they would never know. But apart from themselves, the guanacos and the single horseman, the pampas was empty.

Euan wanted Thia to stay behind and for her dog to stay with her, but Thia would hear nothing of it and Bella was already following the four ostrich dogs across the prairie in the direction of the hunt.

With nowhere to hide on the open pampas there was no option but to continue on. The odds were good – there were eight of them again and only one of him. Hopefully he was not a good shot and would not hit any of them before they were able to surround him or put him or his horse down.

With no dogs to help him, the man was riding erratically, whipping his horse like a man possessed, veering this way and that. Being fixed on his quarry he did not look back and was totally unaware of the approaching riders until they were within fifty yards of him.

Suddenly alarmed, he swivelled in the saddle almost unseating himself. Releasing the reins, he turned his rifle towards the group and fired. The shot went high, but his horse, spurred by the sharp crack and encouraged by the sound of hoofs behind it, galloped even faster.

Davies had the *bolas* in his hand and within a couple of turns all that could be seen of the whirring stone balls was a halo-like circle spinning above his head. Jose also had his *bolas* ready to throw.

'No! He's mine!' Davies yelled.

The man fired again. Missed, and reached for the reins. His only hope was to out-run his pursuers. He spurred his horse viciously but his mount was showing signs of fatigue. It was thin after days of riding and having little adequate grazing.

After six hours in the saddle, the travellers were also tiring, but their horses were still able to respond. Their endurance was remarkable.

With the hiss of an arrow, the whoosh of a condor's wing, the weight and power of a discuss, Davies let the spinning *bolas* fly from his hand. Within the blink of an eye the leather thongs encircled the man's neck and he was knocked from the saddle. His left foot was thrown free but his right boot was firmly fixed in the other silver stirrup. As his leg was wrenched around it twisted his foot driving the spur deep into the horse's flank.

Dragging the man like a limp rag-doll along the ground, the horse kicked and galloped on. For as long as it could feel the vicious spur pressing in its side, it would not stop running.

Davies reined in his horse. The others did likewise. It was a cruel sight but there was nothing they could do and they had no intention of following it through to its conclusion.

After being bounced for miles and miles across the rock-strewn plain, it was unlikely the rider would live to tell his tale. But if the horse eventually settled and returned the man's body back to their camp, with the *bolas* still wound tightly around his neck, the remaining men would know they were being followed. They might think it was the Indians on their trail, but whatever, the fact one of them had been killed would incense them. If they were hungry and their hunting had been unsuccessful, they would be doubly desperate for revenge.

Davies considered the possibilities. The escapees would have two choices: to lie in wait for whoever was pursuing them, or double back and confront them. Not knowing what arms these men were carrying, or what was driving them, a decision had to be made.

Thia and Algernon were eager to go on but Davies and

William were concerned for the weaker members of the English group and for Ana, though she made no comment as usual. There were several hours of daylight left, but, as evening was approaching, it was considered best not to embark on any surprise moves at that hour.

Davies's suggestion, with which the gauchos agreed, was to go after the herd of guanacos which had scattered during the furore.

The dust thrown up by the run-away horse had settled and the plain was now empty apart from themselves and the herd of guanacos. It numbered around a hundred. If they could take two or three animals they could then ride back to the last place they had camped. It was far enough away from danger and they would be assured of a good feed and a peaceful night's sleep. Furthermore there would be time for their horses to graze.

In the morning they could decide what action to take. They could return to the river and give up their search. Or they could continue their efforts to track down the remaining two men. Thia knew that for Davies there was no choice in the matter. This was the second time that luck had been on their side, but they all agreed it was unlikely they would be so fortunate in despatching the other two men.

But despite the positive intentions expressed around the camp-fire, the following morning their spirits were not high. It was not unknown on the pampas for summer to rapidly degenerate into winter and in the morning the rain was pouring down. Under normal circumstances they would have stayed in the camp but they had no intention of letting the Chilotes get far away, nor did they want to be vulnerable by staying in a place the two men could have identified by their camp-fire.

As they rode out, the rain was blowing almost horizontally. The icy wind sweeping down from the Cordillera carried with it the frozen air of the icefields. Soon their clothes were drenched, the icy water stinging their faces. Only Davies and Ana were protected from the wind and rain by the broad fur *capas* fastened around them.

With every ounce of enthusiasm dampened, the riders returned to camp. The visibility was so poor they could not see ahead and would be unable to defend themselves to a surprise attack. Davies said the two men they were following had probably stayed in their camp and it was unlikely the Chilotes would come back looking for them.

It was in a state of disappointment and miserable condition that they stumbled back to their previous campsite. Unfortunately the embers of the morning's fire had completely died but, with the bundles of firewood they were carrying, they were soon able to rekindle the flames. It didn't take long to erect the tents and after drying themselves they crawled under their shelters and waited for the rain to pass.

It had been a wasted day but at least they were able to rest. After a meal of guanaco breast and a fine soup made from a head, Thia and her companions unanimously agreed it was best to stay with Davies despite his suggestion for them to head back to Sandy Point. Not knowing how cunning their prey was, or what behaviour to expect from them, they resolved that their safety depended on them sticking together.

Late that evening as the clouds cleared and the moon shone brightly, the horses suddenly became unsettled. The plaintive tinkling of the *madrinas'* bells could be heard above the neighing and snorting. Davies and the two gauchos leapt up, grabbed their rifles and went out to investigate. Rising from their beds, Thia and her companions followed anxiously.

The horses that had been grazing nearby were agitated, prancing around, circling a stray. Even in the moonlight it was not hard to pick out the intruder which was being challenged by one of the *madrinas*. It was the horse Martin had been riding when they had been caught in the sandstorm. As it turned from them they could see its right flank was blackened with blood and dust, and a silver spur was still lodged in its side. A leather boot was also still entangled in the saddle gear but there was no sign of the man.

Davies spun the *lazo* and dropped it over the mare's head so he could attend to it.

'Tomorrow, the vultures will find where the remains of the man is.'

CHAPTER 19

The Gallegos River

Heading north-east, they were now riding in the opposite direction to Sandy Point. Once they reached the coast, Thia and her companions could sail north to Buenos Ayres or Monte Video. There they would wait for the steamer to take them home to England.

As they were only tracking two men instead of four, Davies was confident they would be able to take them if they could get close enough without being seen. The Chilotes were not expert horsemen and they had no dogs with them for hunting. Soon they would be hungry and have to hunt and it was only going to be a matter of time before they caught up with them.

The next day, the sun proved to be a menace. It was hot and stifling after the rain, and it brought with it a plague of tiny gnats. Having open-necked shirts and sleeves rolled to the elbows, the biting insects managed to penetrate the hidden creases of their body and before long each of them was shuffling uncomfortably in the saddle. But there was no escaping the pests and only evening and a camp-fire brought relief.

'Ahead is the Gallegos River. The Chilotes must cross it. From the other side it is an easy three-day ride to the port. We must stop them before they get there. God only knows what they will do in that town. They will steal whatever goods, clothes and chattels they fancy,' he said. 'It could be a repeat of the '77 Sandy Point massacre!'

'Where will they head from there?'

'If they make it that far, they will take a ship. I don't think they will care which way it is heading. Ships come through fairly often and there are always boats in the harbour; schooners, sealers, fishing boats. If they are desperate enough, they may steal one and attempt to sail it themselves.'

Three hours later, when they reached the well-used ford on the Gallegos River, Davies was shocked. The water was far higher than he had expected. It was swollen, not only by the previous day's rain, but by the melt water from the Cordillera. It had been a particularly long cold winter and the thick snow on the mountains was still thawing. At the ford, the river was 200 yards wide. The current in the centre very strong. If they tried to cross on horseback they would be swept from their horses in the swirling water.

'There is another crossing about ten miles upstream. We may be able to cross there.'

Turning their horses they rode west along the bank following the course of the river, searching for a safe place to cross. As they rode, Davies and the two gauchos searched for tracks left by the pair, but could find none. Thia wondered if the rain had washed them away.

Eventually they reached a straight section of the valley where the river spilled out over a flat plain. On the northern bank tall reeds lined the course and white ibises fished, dipping their beaks into the still-rising water. Califaté bushes dotted with blue berries lined the bank. It looked peaceful.

'We cross here,' Davies said, driving his horse into the shallow water. 'We will camp on the other side. The grazing is good.'

Though the horses were strong and durable, they could not continue to work without good nourishment.

Davies waited as they prepared to cross. Jose, Carlos and Isaac went first leading the baggage horses. Ana followed. She also had a horse in tow. Davies drove the loose horses into the river after them. The level came up to the horses bellies and splashed into the gauchos' fur boots. Thia was followed by her brother and William. The memories of his fall into the icy waters of the ravine made the Englishman nervous.

As they splashed across, the ostrich dogs ran up and down the bank barking. They were not eager to swim the broad expanse of the fast flowing river. But once the gauchos climbed up on to the other bank and called them, they jumped in one after the other and paddled across leaving the Newfoundland stranded on the bank. Sniffing the water, the black dog padded up and down whining.

'Bella,' Thia shouted, turning in her saddle.

'She'll follow,' Davies said.

Thia was concerned. With their webbed feet, Newfoundlands swim extremely well. She had never known her

207

dog to refuse an opportunity before. Something was wrong.

'I must go back for her,' Thia called, turning her horse's head.

But the horse was unwilling to change direction midstream and, as she struggled with it, the saddle girth slipped and she was tipped into the river. Within a few seconds she was under, the swirling water rushing over her head. She struggled and kicked, her boots full of water dragging her down.

A hand grabbed her arm and she felt the solid flanks of a horse rub against her as Davies pulled her up behind him. 'Hold on,' he said.

Shocked and shivering, she grasped her arms around his waist and clung on as his horse fought to swim across the current. As they were carried downstream, Thia glanced to the bank and her heart soared for a moment. Bella was climbing out. She was obviously exhausted and without even shaking herself, she dragged herself towards the bushes on the bank and dropped.

'Bella!' Thia yelled.

The rest of the party crossed successfully but not without incident. One of the pack horses, Thia's horse and several of the spare horses had all been carried away on the current. It was essential that they locate them quickly before they scattered too far.

Five miles downstream where the river made a sweeping curve, they found the animals grazing contentedly. The packhorses still carried their sodden burdens, but Thia's saddle had been swallowed by the river.

Despite the need to press on, it was necessary to make camp, light a fire and allow their boots and the contents of the canvas packs to dry. Isaac went in search of firewood while Carlos and Jose rode off with their dogs in the hope of running down a rhea or surprising a puma. There were plenty of both in the region.

'I must go back for my Bella,' Thia said.

'The dog is safe,' Davies said. 'And when it is rested, it will follow our tracks and find its way here as it did in the wind storm. You must dry yourself. Then eat and sleep. Tomorrow we must ride like the wind.'

After changing her clothes, Thia sat by the fire. Bella had not returned and she prayed that Davies was right. She could not leave in the morning without her.

'Do you miss England?' he asked, when they were alone.

'I miss my father and, surprisingly, I miss my older brother, Horatio. It was wrong of me to deny him the opportunity of coming with us. He would have relished the thrill of this adventure. As for England, there are things I could easily live without. I do not miss the society I am thrown amongst. The ladies moan at the slightest scratch and denigrate their neighbours for not following the latest trends or fashions. They are all preoccupied with wealth and status. The gentlemen are not honest like the Tehuelches who know nothing of greed or envy. The Indians' smile is genuine. They treat their women with respect. And they kill only to survive. It is a sad state that so few of them remain.'

'Do you miss your home?' he said.

'When I look out across the pampas at the endless plain with not a single tree to break the monotony, I sometimes think of the Nottinghamshire woods and forests of Sherwood which back on to Huntingley. I think of the twisted oaks, the elms and ash, and the warm colours of the leaves in autumns carpeting the ground. Then I think of England in mid-winter and the bare branches; stark, cold and silent. Then my mind returns to this place. It has a calling of its own. It stirs the heart and soul – that is the only way I can describe it.'

CHAPTER 20

Face to Face with Evil

It was dawn and everything was wet. Thia had listened to the rain through the night thundering on the tarpaulin above her head. Without her dog sleeping against her legs, she had felt cold.

From the open end of the tent, Thia could see Carlos attempting to re-ignite the embers of the previous evening's fire. Davies was striding down to the river with a towel in his hand. Isaac was on the bank already, washing the iron cooking pot. Jose was nowhere in sight, but he would be about somewhere, perhaps cutting some meat for breakfast. From the next tent she could hear her brother snoring and was certain that William, who liked to sleep late, was probably still asleep also.

Davies's words were ringing in her head: *we must leave early if we are to catch these men. We must ride like the wind.* He had assured her that her Newfoundland would find its way to the camp, but Bella had not come back. It was a three-day ride from the Gallegos River to Port Saint Julian and, irrespective

211

of what happened on the way, when they arrived in the town they would board a ship and sail north to Monte Video. She knew they would not be coming back and was afraid she would never see her dog again.

If Davies knew her intention was to search the river-bank for her Newfoundland, he would stop her. This was her last chance. She must find her.

Slipping on her britches and boots, Thia picked up her rifle and slipped out from under the far end of the tent. Staying low behind the califaté bushes and moving stealthily, she kept well away from the horses. They were intelligent and alert and always quick to announce anything unusual. She had formulated her plan overnight and decided to go on foot, that way she could conduct a better search and would hear any sound her dog made. She considered they had only ridden a couple of miles downstream from where Bella had climbed out.

But the image of the Newfoundland being carried along by the current, emerging from the water exhausted, struggling up the bank and collapsing, was still foremost in her mind. The breed was renowned for its strong swimming ability and its endurance. Why hadn't Bella obeyed when she had called her? Had the water seeped into her lungs? Was she dying? Thia was afraid. If she was ill or injured, the smell of her wet hair could attract a prowling puma. A weak dog would be easy prey for a big cat.

Thia thought about the Chilotes. The day was only just dawning and in her mind it was unlikely the two men would hurry. She knew Bella was somewhere on the river's edge between their overnight camp and the ford. It would take no more than an hour to get there and back and she had promised herself she would find her pet, even if she was dead.

Hurrying along the bank, Thia was amazed how much the water had risen overnight. It was considerably deeper than when they had crossed and the fast flowing channel in the middle was no longer merely corrugated with ripples on the surface, it rolled in sweeps like waves on the ocean. How relieved she was that they had crossed the previous day.

The sun came up and she felt it warm on her back. It was warming the land too and a mist was rising from the wet earth blanketing the pampas in cloud tinged with pink. The water birds were already busy in the shallows. Having run until all the air in her lungs was exhausted, she slowed and picked a handful of ripe berries from the bushes on the bank.

Glancing through the river's mist she detected movement at the other side. A small group of guanacos, maybe? Then she saw them. Two riders with two pack horses following them. They were riding west towards the ford. Thia dropped to her haunches. They had not seen her.

The two Chilotes, having ridden too far east had found the river impossible to cross. Now they were following the same route she and her companions had taken the previous day. They were obviously still searching for a safe place to cross.

Ducking behind the bushes, not daring to move until they were well past, Thia's heart pounded as she waited. She was fearful of being seen but knew she must run and tell Euan and the others. The minutes seemed like hours as she watched the horses heading silently upstream on the opposite side of the river.

When she felt satisfied that the men were far enough away and unlikely to look back, she got up cautiously. As she did, she heard a faint whining sound. She listened intently. Was it one of the water birds? They often made strange and alarming noises especially in the night.

'Bella,' she shouted softly, fearing her voice would carry across the Gallegos.

There was no response.

'Where are you, Bella?'

Nothing. Standing bolt upright she scanned the river-bank. Fifty yards upstream in a low hollow beneath the entangled branches of a califaté bush she saw her Newfoundland but the dog was no longer black. Her straggly hair was the colour of wet pampas dust.

'Come, Bella!' she called, as loudly as she dare.

The dog lifted its head but did not rise.

Thia wanted to rush over, hug her pet and take her back, but the Chilotes were riding almost opposite the spot where the Newfoundland was sheltering.

Knowing Bella would be cold and hungry, but satisfied in the knowledge she was alive, Thia called out, 'Stay there, girl, I'll come back for you.'

Carlos was strong. He could carry her or they could make a stretcher to transport her on.

Splashing through the reeds on the river's edge and slipping on the muddy banks, Thia ran as fast as she could.

'Euan!' she yelled, as she neared the campsite.

'Thank God you are safe,' Euan cried, as he came out to greet her.

'Those men are across the other side. They are heading for the ford. And I have found Bella!'

While Jose went to round up the horses which had wandered about a mile away, William insisted Thia settle herself and eat some breakfast. But she was too excited and the califaté berries were all she could stomach.

'I will take Jose and Carlos with me,' Davies said. 'The rest of you will stay here. These men will stop at nothing. It will be no picnic. You can get your dog when all of this is over.'

Thia desperately wanted to go with him, but was convinced to stay in the camp with her companions.

When Jose returned, they saddled their horses. Armed with rifles, revolvers, *bolas* and the curved daggers stuck down the back of their belts, they were ready.

'Where is Ana?' Euan called.

No one had missed her. Perhaps she was further down the river. She always liked to bathe in privacy.

'When she returns, tell her to stay with you.' Davies spurred his horse and, with the two gauchos, headed upstream towards the ford.

Algernon made Thia a bowl of oatmeal. William added wood to the fire. Isaac draped the furs over the bushes. It was an opportunity to dry their clothes but in their anxiety they lacked enthusiasm. Sitting by the camp-fire with their hands wrapped around pots of coffee they watched the river flowing by. At times a bush or log, carried down from the forests in the foothills of the Cordillera, bobbed on the current. They watched it pass.

'There!' Thia screamed, pointing to the centre of the river.

They immediately saw it. A horse, battling the strong current was being carried downstream. Only its head was visible and at times the waves were washing over it.

'See behind it. A man clinging to the tail!' William shouted.

All eyes were on the head bobbing in the water. No one could see the man's face, but they all recognized the distinctive bowler hat fixed firmly on his head.

Thia jumped to her feet and reached for her rifle. It was loaded.

'No!' shouted William. 'Don't do it.'

As he spoke, the man lost his grip. Flailing his arms, he was carried along for a few yards before disappearing.

The black hat, floating like a rudderless coracle, continued its journey to the sea.

Thia shook her head. 'They must have attempted to swim the horses at the ford but the water is now too fast and deep. Perhaps the other man is also in the river.' Then she realized. 'Euan is riding for the ford. He may not have seen them drift by. We must go and tell him!'

Two miles upstream Ana was standing alone on the river-bank. She was clutching a skinning knife.

No one had noticed her slip out when Thia returned to the camp with the news of the men. No one heard her approach a horse. No one saw her throw a *lazo* over its neck and spring up on to its bare back. No one heard her ride off.

When she caught sight of the men riding at the other side of the river, she followed them. When they eventually reached the ford, she slid from her horse and stood on the bank waiting.

When the two riders approached the crossing, their horses refused to go in. The men tried several places along the bank but all with the same result. Finally, angry and frustrated they backed up. Using whip and spur, they galloped the horses straight into the water.

Though the water was deep, the current at the edges was not strong, but the horses soon lost their footing and had to swim. The two men were still seated but the force of water rushing between them and their saddles was lifting them.

The first to slip off was the man wearing the bowler hat. Ana recognized it. He flailed his arms in desperation and managed to grab hold of the horse's tail.

The second man ignored him. He, too, was being carried downstream but was urging his horse to swim towards the middle of the channel.

Ana knew the man had seen her, but she didn't care.

Walking quickly, she kept pace with the flow.

Mid-way across, the water swirled violently. The man, lying flat along his horse's neck, held on as long as he could but it was not long before he too was dislodged. He grabbed the mane and clung on, but the current sucked him under the horse's head and washed him away. The horse was swept around till it was facing the bank from which it had come. It started swimming back.

Paddling desperately, the man stayed afloat and swam towards the edge where Ana was waiting for him.

Dragging himself from the water, dripping wet, he remained stooped over for a moment till he regained his breath.

'You waiting for me?' he said, as he lifted his face. He had only one eye. 'Come,' he said, beckoning her, an evil smile on his face.

As she stepped forward, he pulled a revolver from his belt. Cocked it and pointed. Only three paces separated the pair.

'No,' shouted Davies, his rifle sights set on the man.

The man glanced up as the rifle cracked, the shot taking the revolver from his hand and his thumb with it.

When he dropped into the shallows, the river flowed red around him.

Ana stepped forward.

'No,' Davies said. 'It is done.'

With their prisoner securely bound and watched constantly by at least one of them, they stayed at the camp on the river-bank for another night.

In the afternoon, Jose and Carlos went hunting and caught their last guanaco. It would provide sufficient meat to last for the next three days.

'Your business is complete now, is it not?' Thia said, when she was alone with the Welshman.

'It is,' he said. 'I shall take this one to town and let the authorities deal with him.'

That night he built a small fire on the river's edge.

From a distance, the English travellers watched as he and Ana finally said farewell to Kattn. The Indian woman wailed as was the custom and as the sparks rose into the night sky Euan placed the long plait of jet black hair on to the flames. It frizzled, sending a distinctive smell drifting over the camp.

Later in the evening, when the others had retired and the small fire was almost dead, Thia wandered down to the water and asked the Welshman if she might join him.

Gazing at the southern sky, he was holding the condor's feather in his hand.

'At last her spirit is free,' Thia said.

'Yes,' he replied.

CHAPTER 21

The Condor's Feather

Riding away from the Gallegos River, the scenery was similar to that which they had been travelling through for the last 300 miles. It was barren and inhospitable and as unchanging as a silent sea.

At times Thia had wished for home, for the genteel refinement of afternoon tea in the drawing-room, elegantly served from a silver pot. How different it was to the communal pot of maté which was passed around each evening – everyone drinking from the same container. But the green leafy drink was so refreshing. She must buy a sack of leaves in Port Saint Julian to take back to England.

She thought about Davies: the quiet stranger she had first seen on the docks at Liverpool. A man who had carried so much anger and sadness. The man who had guided them across the vast pampas of Patagonia. They had seen the Cordillera, the beechwood forests, the peat swamps, the ravines. They had climbed up from one plateau to another and then descended the steppes across the huge expanse of Patagonia.

This was no country like any other she had read about. It was a wild place filled with silence and wind. Here the land alone was supreme. In the west, the Cordillera's dagger-like peaks jutted from the horizon – a picket fence of stone arrowheads confronting the giants who climbed the staircase of plateaux stretching the full width of South America.

Thia had seen the lakes resplendent in their colours, pink, purple, metallic blue, and the shimmering white of the salt lakes. She had seen the birds, the pink flamingos, the crested waterbirds, the ibises. And she had seen the condors riding on the thermals and remembered the black feather which the Welshman always carried.

She had seen the animals, the fast running rheas which could double back quicker than any African ostrich, the foxes, the desert rats and the proud guanaco without whose meat and skins they would have not survived their journey.

She wondered if she would ever see these things again. If she would ever step on the soil of this forgotten part of the world. She promised herself she would.

They were in no hurry as they headed north to Port Saint Julian. On the second day, they disturbed an ostrich sitting on a clutch of eggs. The roasted eggs, flavoured with a dash of sugar, made a delicious addition to their diet.

Almost a week later, when they rode into the small harbour town, Thia felt a sense of relief. But there was also disappointment. Their journey had come to an end. They would stay in the town only until they could board a ship. With a number of vessels anchored in the harbour, it was likely that would not be long.

Davies's face was almost as deeply tanned as that of the gauchos as he led the horse with his prisoner aboard to the gaol. He was content to hand the escapee to the authorities. No doubt news of the atrocities the Chilotes had committed recently would have already reached the town and without the protection of the gaol, his life would be worth nothing. He should consider himself lucky if he was returned to the prison in Buenos Ayres.

As they rode down the street searching for accommodation and a stable for the horses, Thia and her companions attracted attention from the locals. It was not unusual for hunters to come in from the pampas, or Indians to pass through, but they had never seen an Englishwoman whose clothes were torn and dishevelled, with hair plaited and tied with a hank of spun guanaco fleece. Thia didn't think about her appearance. She was proud of what they had achieved and the ordeals they had survived.

Of the two English gentlemen riding beside her, one wore a fur *capa* over his shirt. It was fastened at the neck by a silver clasp. His blond flowing locks were held in place by a coloured fillet fastened around his forehead. Riding bareback beside him was a full-blood Tehuelche Indian. Algernon sat proudly in the saddle. Isaac followed him and Jose and Carlos rode behind with their four hunting dogs trotting alongside.

Bella, dusty, weary and dishevelled, padded faithfully next to Thia. Perched behind her on the horse's back was a wicker basket, the type the Tehuelche Indian women carried their infants in. Ana had collected the reeds on the river-bank and woven it for her. Sleeping in a warm nest of soft guanaco fur were five still-blind Newfoundland pups.

On the short dock, William stood beside Ana but they did not

221

touch or speak to each other.

'I will ride with Ana,' William said. 'I want to see more of the pampas. Visit her people. I want to paint. Sketch the flora and fauna. And draw the faces of the Tehuelche Indians. I want to see the Cordillera dressed in its sable mantle and one day I will return to England with these images for everyone to see.'

What his future was with Ana, he did not say.

There were tears in Algy's eyes as he prepared to board the schooner and say goodbye to his dearest friend. 'You never did teach me the intricacies of chess,' he said, forcing a smile. 'You must come back to England soon and honour that wager.'

'Don't worry, I will. But I must live this dream for a little longer yet. Take care.' William said, hugging his friend. 'Now you have proved you can cook you must visit me in Mayfair when I return.'

Algernon laughed. 'I'm afraid we will soon starve. My expertise only extends to ostrich and guanaco meat.'

'Goose and venison are not very different, so you will have no excuses. *Adieu*, Algy,' William said, tears glistening in his eyes.

Thia smiled at her brother and his travelling companion. They had journeyed so far together and now none of them wanted their journey to end.

With a gloved hand, she tossed back her wiry hair but the sea breeze blew it across her face. Around her neck, the creamy-white Swiss lace accentuated the rich tan of her skin. The deep blue of the evening sky was reflected in her dress's sash. She felt slightly uncomfortable after wearing breeches for so many weeks.

'My dearest Thia,' William said. 'This adventure has been

the most wonderful experience of my whole life, one I will never forget. And,' he said, with a grin, 'if you ever become desperate for a husband, I would always be willing to present myself to Lord Beresford for consideration.'

'Oh, William,' Thia said, smiling. 'You are so sweet. That is the first and only proposal I have ever received and I will always remember it.'

'God speed you on your journey,' he said.

'And to you and Ana. I know she is dear to you.'

Thia kissed her friend then pressed her head to the Indian's forehead and kissed her lightly on the cheek.

There were tears of gratitude in Ana's dark eyes as she lifted her hand and waved farewell.

As the Steam Navigations Company's ship weighed anchor and sailed, Thia stood on the deck watching the Patagonian sky as it changed through pink to orange then finally gold, the layers of colour falling over each other in that familiar concertina which closed very slowly to squeeze out the last traces of every day.

Now the mountains and ridges of the Cordillera were far far away and she wondered if she would ever return.

She had left so much behind.

Byron – her father's beloved Newfoundland, buried amongst the beechwood thickets on the edge of the prairie.

Euan Davies – the enigmatic stranger she had come to know. A man she now admired. A man who intrigued her as no man before had ever done. How different he looked with his moustache gone and his face as brown and bare as that of a Tehuelche Indian. She had begged him to sail with them to England but he had things to attend to and had ridden back to the pampas, the place he regarded as his home.

But more – she had left something of her heart in Patagonia. And she had grown from her experience. She had learned how to share. Learned how the care of others was more important than satisfying her own selfish whims. She had learned that an animal could be sacrificed for food but not for sport. She had experienced the freedom of the vast pampas where there were no fences or barriers but where life and death was a struggle every single day. And she had admired the spirit of the Criollo horses without whose courage and endurance they could never have succeeded in their journey.

In her hand she clutched the condor's feather which Euan had given her before he rode away.

'Hold this for me and keep it safe,' he said. 'I will be returning to England before the southern winter sets in and I will come to Huntingley to retrieve it.'

Knowing its significance to him, she was sure he would keep his promise.

Perhaps one day they would sail back to Patagonia together to gallop across the open pampas, climb the high plateaux, swim the rivers and reach the elusive snow-capped peaks which forever seemed just a day's ride away.